A
DICKENS
OF A CHRISTMAS

Jerry Wolfrom

Beverly Justice

Samuel O Basket

Dick Masters

Jam Clap

Joy L. W. Erskine

Dwain Willins

Martha Jumail

Beverly Kerr

Rick Booth

A DICKENS

OF A CHRISTMAS

RAINY DAY WRITERS
CAMBRIDGE, OHIO

A Dickens of a Christmas
ISBN-13: 978-1492342663
ISBN-10: 1492342661

RAINY DAY WRITERS
CAMBRIDGE, OHIO

TABLE OF CONTENTS

Acknowledgments

A Dickens of a Christmas comes in response to repeated requests for another book of Rainy Day Writers' Christmas stories. Our first was *Cambridge at Christmastime*, a collection of short stories about coming home to Cambridge for the holidays. In *A Dickens of a Christmas*, we shift our focus to the Dickens Village scenes that populate Wheeling Avenue during the holiday season each year—did you know that each has a story to tell?

In typical over-the-top Rainy Day fashion, we launched this project with a photo session at the Dickens Welcome Center, where we donned Victorian-era clothing and were transported in spirit to the time of Charles Dickens and Tiny Tim. Though it was mid-summer, our holiday enthusiasm bloomed like poinsettias on Christmas Day.

Shortly thereafter, we were treated to an afternoon tour of Dickens Universal, a magical place where Dickens characters are pampered during the off-season like the Queen's corgi. Costumes are cleaned, repaired, or replaced; faces scrubbed and painted; and all is refreshed and refurbished. The Rainy Day Writers took copious notes and lots of pictures to aid the storytelling process. True to form, we also "made" great new friends during this visit, whom you will meet elsewhere in this book (see pages 188-189).

From those summer beginnings to the realization of this Christmas publication, it's been an arduous process, but we've enjoyed putting our thoughts on paper for you to enjoy.

To all who helped make it possible, we extend our heartfelt thanks. Special appreciation is due the Board of Directors of Dickens Victorian Village, particularly to Jonett Haberfield and Harriette Orr for coordinating access to the Dickens Welcome Center and Dickens Universal, and to Bob Ley and Jonett Haberfield for the historical chronology shared in their twin forewords for this book.

We also express our gratitude to Michael Neilson Photography. Mike's willingness and exceptional photographic aptitude makes our ragged bunch look pretty dang good; to *The Daily and Sunday Jeffersonian* for their support in promoting the Rainy Day Writers in the community; to Crossroads Library for lending space for our notoriously noisy meetings; to Joy Erskine for her untiring dedication to publishing *A Dickens of a Christmas*; to Mr. Lee's Restaurant for great food and a pleasant place to gather and unwind; and to all the other local businesses who support us by offering our books for sale.

Finally, we extend our love and appreciation to our loyal readers, who continue to support and sustain our every effort. You give us reason to keep on writing.

Bringing Home the Tree—*The "man of the house" would have brought home a tree for decoration. Charles Dickens' boyhood was spent in various residences around London and Kent, owing to his father John's occupation as a clerk in the Navy Pay Office.*

ONE MAN'S DREAM, AND A COMMUNITY THAT MADE IT HAPPEN!

BOB LEY

As lifelong business people in downtown Cambridge, my wife, Sue, and I had been talking about drawing more people to our beautiful downtown. After a Christmastime visit to the *Winter Festival of Lights* in Wheeling, the conversation again turned to building traffic for downtown Cambridge. What could Cambridge do that might capture some of the visitors going to Wheeling? Traffic streamed past us on the way to Wheeling from the north, from the south, and from the west.

"Something that could be enjoyed both days and evenings."

"Our architecture is definitely Victorian."

"Cambridge history is definitely English."

"Why not a Charles Dickens tribute to *A Christmas Carol?*"

I am an amateur artist and a born tinkerer. I had spent nearly fifty years in the clothing business. I reread the book, then started making drawings for scenes, realizing that to sell this idea it would have to be well thought out. I am familiar with mannequins so I spent a few nights in my workshop designing and building a life-size mannequin that would be reasonable to build and could be easily posed.

I took 'Charlie,' my first prototype mannequin, to a Cambridge Main Street meeting. I was allowed to present my idea, along with "Charlie" (who was "sitting" in a chair beside me) and my drawings. I had lined up a few people skilled in areas I was not: travel, sculpting, and so on.

There were seventeen people at the meeting. I knew we had a potential success when sixteen volunteered to serve on the committee. The idea struck a chord. I had never asked for volunteers before and sixteen out of seventeen hands went up.

The mayor was there and offered us $2,000 in start-up money and a large room in which to begin. It wasn't long before we had outgrown the room and the Edgetech Corporation came through with a terrific space of 5,000 square feet at the right price...free!

We kept the media informed. We asked for the scenes to be sponsored and our citizens came through, like they always do. We were getting the money to proceed! Donations large and small were coming in and continue to come in every year.

Truly successful ideas almost always happen because good people make them happen. Cambridge was lucky to have skilled artists from the Eastern Ohio Art Guild, who agreed to make the heads. One of their charter members chaired this project and sculpted more than a hundred heads. They put in countless hours of trial-and-error work, arriving finally at the incredible finished products now on display. Their expressions are priceless!

Meanwhile, a cadre of men met several nights a week for months, building platforms and doing all kinds of odd jobs.

Mid-East Career and Technology Center volunteered to build a hundred mannequins! We furnished the lumber and a blueprint in January and they called in May and said, "Finished!"

Women from all walks of life showed up to dress them, using Victorian catalogues for guidance. Bonnets, capes, and long skirts were made. Tuxedoes were transformed into Edwardian clothes for the gents. They were then assembled on the platforms, ready to be positioned on Wheeling Avenue.

Again the media came through, trumpeting our need for flatbed trailers, trucks, and volunteers. Several hundred showed up the first Sunday. Our committee was overwhelmed with help and the scenes were on the street within hours.

We held our collective breath for the entire season. *What would snow do to them? Or high winds? Would vandalism be a problem? Would people come to see them?*

The snow only made them more beautiful. They survived the Ohio winter in fine style. One of our few instances of vandalism happened the first year. Three men with too much Christmas spirits knocked down seven mannequins. Fortunately, a citizen reported it to the police, who captured and arrested the fellows. They spent Christmas in jail! A friend remarked, "From the townspeople's reaction, it might have been better if they had kidnapped the Pope!"

Would people come to see them? You bet they would! Downtown Cambridge looked like Christmastime in the Fifties. People were downtown day and night, taking pictures. Families came and walked the streets, reading the brass plaques at each scene. They called relatives and friends and made repeat visits. The shops were humming. Parking was packed. Merchants reported great things for the season.

One former resident upon her Christmas return offered, "It makes me so proud to say I am from Cambridge. *Our* town did this!" And I have to say I'm pretty proud of us myself.

A Christmas Feast—*Preparations for a traditional British Christmas meal began several days in advance. A typical meal might consist of port jelly, oyster stuffing, plum pudding, and mincemeat pies. Regional preference determined whether the meat served would be goose, beef, or turkey.*

THE MOST UNIQUE HOLIDAY DESTINATION IN THE MIDWEST

JONETT HABERFIELD

As a steward of tourism and former tour operator, I was honored to be invited to share Bob Ley's vision for creating a tourism destination in Historic Downtown Cambridge. From the beginning, we knew that whatever we created had to be unique and special enough to bring visitors, while also building pride amongst our residents.

"Charlie's" companion, "Sarabelle," spent many hours touring the county with me and the Visitors and Convention Bureau staff. While our volunteers worked tirelessly to make Bob's vision a reality, we promoted our little holiday project to tour operators at trade shows. As interest grew, so did our excitement.

The first season, we had an incredible *dozen* motor coaches visit Cambridge to see what they'd been hearing about. They spent money at the restaurants, the hotels, the downtown shops, and many of the other attractions in the area. Each tour was and still is guided by a volunteer in costume, who shares our incredible story, volunteer spirit, and local history. To date, we have welcomed more than 47 motor coaches in a single season! Our volunteer tour guides empowered tour bus passengers to become our "word of mouth" advertisers by telling everyone they know about their experience in Cambridge. And as a result, visitors arriving by car have been tenfold.

By year three, it was clear that an official Dickens Welcome Center was needed to share our story, dispense our Visitor's Guide, and offer an opportunity for individuals and families to immerse themselves in our unique holiday destination. This center is staffed by volunteers. The Welcome Center offers souvenirs, a tea room, and the very popular Imagination Station, where visitors put costumes over their clothes and pose for pictures around the beautiful Victorian Christmas tree, in the window with Charles Dickens at his desk, or with the Duke and Duchess of Cambridge.

The addition of the Guernsey County Courthouse Music & Light Show has been a true blessing for both the Dickens Victorian Village and the City of Cambridge. A gift from a local resident and prominent businessman, Grant Hafley, this spectacular display has become a tradition and source of pride for local residents.

2012 brought the addition of many new programs, including trolley rides and "The Educational Side of Dickens." Created by a group of retired teachers, this educational field trip welcomed 800+ students in the inaugural year.

As we continue to grow and improve each year, we strive to meet the needs of a changing traveling public. Our mission is to create a destination with an Old World atmosphere that preserves history through education, creates memories, and develops family traditions. Improvements to our website, the addition of "themed" weekends, and events that cater to a variety of demographics are what keep our destination fresh and exciting. The endless dedication of our volunteers and our natural "hometown hospitality" warms the hearts of visitors, who continue to spread the word about "The Most Unique Holiday Destination in the Midwest."

$$\maltese\, \mathfrak{R}D\mathfrak{W}\mathcal{S}$$

"Every traveler has a home of his own, and he learns to appreciate it the more from his wandering."

~ Charles Dickens.

He's Been Here—*"I will honour Christmas in my heart, and try to keep it all the year, I will live in the Past, the Present, and the Future. The Spirits of all three shall strive within me. I will not shut out the lessons that they teach."—Charles Dickens*

Charles Dickens,
A Lifetime of Great Writing

JERRY WOLFROM

Charles Dickens was born on February 7, 1812, in Landport, Portsea, England, to John and Elizabeth Dickens. Dickens' father was a clerk stricken with poverty and debt, which kept the Dickens family moving from one unfavorable location to the next. Dickens was the second of eight children, two of whom died in childhood.

A frail child, Charles took to bookishness early. As a boy, he never attended a real school; at first, he attended a "homemade" school run by local women, then, for two years until the age of nine, he attended a school run by a Baptist minister.

In 1821, the Dickens family moved to London, where Charles experienced what was probably the darkest period of his childhood. John Dickens sank deeper into debt until he was thrown into Marshalsea Prison as a debtor. Shortly thereafter, Mrs. Dickens and the children were forced to move into the prison with him.

Work was found for Charles as a label-paster at a blacking factory, with coworkers of the lowest type. He lived in a small room nearby, visiting the prison on Sundays. Charles hated his situation and lived in misery during this time.

Finally, the Dickens family left the prison. Charles went to a standard school from age twelve to fourteen. At fourteen, he became an attorney's office boy. There he began his first study of the law, which would lead to his great knowledge of and contempt for it, as his works demonstrate.

Dickens' first success as a writer came just as he married Catherine Hogarth. The first portion of his *Pickwick Papers*, a serialized novel, was published two days before his marriage and went on to become a big success.

Eight children were eventually born to the Dickens'. Charles became the editor of a new magazine where "Oliver Twist," as well as several other works, first appeared.

His interest in the theater led him to write four plays that received only modest reviews. In 1840, Dickens came to America, but the scourge of slavery, as well as disputes over copyright laws, led to his departure in June 1842.

In 1845, the height of Dickens' fame came with the publication of *David Copperfield*, considered by many to be Dickens' greatest work.

On June 9, 1870, while working on *The Mystery of Edwin Drood* in London, Dickens died. He was mourned by a grateful nation and was buried alongside England's other great writers in Westminster Abbey in London. Following are brief comments on some of Dickens' work.

A CHRISTMAS CAROL

A Christmas Carol is a novella first published on December 19, 1843. The story tells of sour and miserly Ebenezer Scrooge's ideological, ethical, and emotional transformation, resulting from supernatural visits from Jacob Marley and the Ghosts of Christmas Past, Present, and Yet to Come. The novella met instant success and critical acclaim, igniting a new interest in Christmas around the world.

The book was written and published in early Victorian Era Britain, a period when there was both strong nostalgia for old Christmas traditions and an initiation of new practices, such as Christmas trees and greeting cards. Dickens' sources for the tale appear to be many and varied but are principally the humiliating experiences of his childhood, his sympathy for the poor, and various Christmas stories.

The tale has been viewed by critics as an indictment of 19th Century industrial capitalism.

The story has been credited with restoring the holiday to one of merriment and festivity in Britain and America, after a period of sobriety and somberness. *A Christmas Carol* remains popular; has never been out of print; and has been adapted to film, stage, opera, and television.

DAVID COPPERFIELD

David Copperfield is probably the most autobiographical Dickens novel. He uses many incidents of his childhood and early life to create a considerable fictional achievement.

David Copperfield is also the novel that stands as a midpoint in Dickens' oeuvre—somewhat indicative of Dickens' work. This novel contains a complicated plot structure, a concentration on the moral and social worlds, and some of Dickens' most wonderful comic creations. *David Copperfield* is a broad canvas on which the great master of Victorian fiction uses his entire palette. Unlike many of Dickens' other novels, however, *David Copperfield* is written from the point of view of its titular character, seemingly looking back on the ups and downs of his long life.

A TALE OF TWO CITIES

Set in London and Paris, this Dickens novel covers Paris before and during the French Revolution. With well over 200 million copies sold, it ranks among the most famous works in the history of fictional literature.

The novel depicts the plight of the French peasantry demoralized by the French aristocracy in the years leading up to the revolution, the corresponding brutality demonstrated by the revolutionaries toward the former aristocrats in the early years of the revolution, and many unflattering social parallels with life in London during the same time period.

It follows the lives of several protagonists through these events. The most notable are Charles Darnay and Sydney Carton. Darnay is a former French aristocrat who falls victim to the indiscriminate wrath of the revolution despite his virtuous nature, and Carton is a dissipated English barrister who endeavors to redeem his ill-spent life out of his love for Darnay's wife.

The 45-chapter novel was published in 31 weekly installments in Dickens' new literary periodical, *All The Year Round*, from April 1859 to November 1859.

OLIVER TWIST

Oliver Twist, subtitled *The Parish Boy's Progress*, was Charles Dickens' second novel. The story is about an orphan, Oliver Twist, who endures a miserable existence in a workhouse, then is placed with an undertaker. He escapes and travels to London, where he meets the Artful Dodger, leader of a gang of juvenile pickpockets. Naively unaware of their unlawful activities, Oliver is led to the lair of their elderly criminal trainer, Fagin.

Oliver Twist is notable for Dickens' unromantic portrayal of criminals and their sordid lives. Exposed is the cruel treatment of many a waif-child in London, which increased international concern in what is known as "The Great London Waif Crisis," the large number of orphans in London in the Dickens era.

An early example of the social novel, it calls attention to various contemporary evils, including child labor, the recruitment of children as criminals, and the presence of street children. Dickens mocks the hypocrisies of his time by surrounding the novel's serious themes with sarcasm and dark humor.

Most literature experts believe it likely Dickens' own early youth as a child laborer contributed to the story's development. The book has been the subject of numerous film and television adaptations, and the basis for a highly successful musical play.

GREAT EXPECTATIONS

Dickens' classic story, *Great Expectations*, is full of meaning. It is all about the deep and touching life of a boy named Pip. At the start of the book, we discover that Pip is a young boy who has no parents. His parents and siblings have passed away through reasons unknown to the reader. He is left to his sister, Mrs. Joe, to be brought up, rather painfully, "by hand." Luckily, she is not the only one to bring him up, as she is married to a blacksmith, Joe, who is Pip's friend and guide throughout his life.

Dickens portrays his characters and develops them through their lives in an incredibly amazing way. Each character plays an important part in Pip's life and many of them were enduring associates, such as "the pale young gentleman" that Pip fought in the courtyard at the Satis House, who turned out to be Herbert, the young man with whom Pip shares a room at Barnard's Inn. The return of Abel Magwitch, the convict, as Pip's benefactor was very astonishing! All these characters, and the brilliant way they are developed and related to Pip, shed a light of understanding on the mood of the story.

Although this book is full of pleasantry and familiarity, it is also filled with difficulties and conflicts for Pip. The main conflict in this story is "man versus himself." The reader can see that Pip has a strong conscience and wishes to improve himself.

THE MYSTERY OF EDWIN DROOD

This is Dickens' final novel. It was unfinished at the time of Dickens' death in June 1870 and his ending for it remains unknown. Consequently, the identity of the murderer remains subject to debate.

Though the novel is named after the character Edwin Drood, the story focuses on Drood's uncle, choirmaster John Jasper, who is in love with his pupil, Rosa Bud. Miss Bud is Drood's fiancée, who is also admired by the high-spirited and hot-tempered Neville Landless, who comes from Ceylon with his twin sister, Helena. Landless and Drood take an instant dislike to one another. Drood later disappears under mysterious circumstances.

The story is set in Cloisterham, a lightly disguised Rochester. Mr. Crisparkle, for example, lives in a clergy house in Minor Canon Corner, which corresponds to a genuine address within the precincts of Rochester Cathedral, namely Minor Canon Row.

Years later, the story was turned into a blockbuster musical. There, the audience finished the story, Dickens didn't. It was the only show in New York that ended differently every night, depending on what the audience decided. The cast included Stephanie J. Block (*Anything Goes*), Will Chase (*Smash*), Gregg Edelman (*Wonderful Town*), Jim Norton (*The Seafarer*), and Chita Rivera (*Nine*). The rollicking presentation earned a Tony for best musical, best book, and best score.

CHARLES DICKENS
A MAN BLESSED WITH AMAZING TALENT

JERRY WOLFROM

Charles Dickens was a prolific writer whose work is called episodic because most of his books were published as serials in magazines and newspapers before he assembled them into book form.

Below is a list of his best-known works:

- *The Posthumous Papers of the Pickwick Club* (Monthly serial, April 1836 to November 1837).
- *The Adventures of Oliver Twist* (Monthly serial in *Bentley's Miscellany*, February 1837 to April 1839).
- *The Life and Adventures of Nicholas Nickleby* (Monthly serial, April 1838 to October 1839).
- *The Old Curiosity Shop* (Weekly serial in *Master Humphrey's Clock*, 25 April 1840 to 6 February 1841).
- *Barnaby Rudge: A Tale of the Riots of 'Eighty* (Weekly serial in *Master Humphrey's Clock*, 13 February 1841 to 27 November 1841).
- *The Life and Adventures of Martin Chuzzlewit* (Monthly serial, January 1843 to July 1844).
- *A Christmas Carol*, in *The Chimes* (1844)
- *The Cricket on the Hearth* (1845)
- *The Battle of Life* (1846)

- *The Haunted Man and the Ghost's Bargain* (1848).
- *Dombey and Son* (Monthly serial, October 1846 to April 1848).
- *David Copperfield* (Monthly serial, May 1849 to November 1850).
- *Bleak House* (Monthly serial, March 1852 to September 1853).
- *Hard Times: For These Times* (Weekly serial in *Household Words*, 1 April 1854 to 12 August 1854).
- *Little Dorrit* (Monthly serial, December 1855 to June 1857).
- *A Tale of Two Cities* (Weekly serial in *All the Year Round*, 30 April 1859 to 26 November 1859).
- *Great Expectations* (Weekly serial in *All the Year Round*, December 1860 to August 1861).
- *Our Mutual Friend* (Monthly serial, May 1864 to November 1865).
- *The Mystery of Edwin Drood* (Monthly serial, April 1870 to September 1870. Only six of twelve planned numbers completed).

THE
STORIES

The Photographer—*Astronomer John Herschel first used the term photography in 1839 when his British friend, William Fox Talbot invented light-sensitive paper. The photographer mannequin was fashioned after local photographer Michael Neilson. His subject's face is that of Pittsburgh, Pennsylvania resident, Judy McGarry.*

"SAY CHEESE"

BEVERLY J. JUSTICE

It was Dina's fault. She always tended bar at the Blue Jay on Tuesday nights. If only she had not traded her days with Tyrone, then Doug and Ray Sowers would not have been kicked out of the bar.

"I told you to leave that blonde alone!" scolded Ray. "She's way out of your league."

"How was I to know that she was Tyrone's sister? He's as ugly as a bulldog sucking a lemon and she's an eleven on a scale of one to ten. No family resemblance there!"

"And you had to use that stupid line: 'Those must be mirror jeans because I can see myself in them.' Doug, I swear your I.Q. drops ten points with every beer you drink."

"Whatever, dude. We've got a half-mile walk home and it's only twenty-eight degrees. At least that's what the guy on TV said before Tyrone tossed us out the door."

"It is cold," agreed Ray. "And it's starting to snow. Let's take a shortcut down Wheeling Avenue."

"O-oh, I don't know, man," Doug answered, stopping in his tracks. "It's one o'clock in the morning and those—those 'people' are all over the place."

Ray tilted back in a hearty laugh. "My big brother, Fearless Doug, is afraid of the Victorian mannequins? That's a good one!"

"Laugh all you want! Those things are freaky. They have eyes that stare right through you. And sometimes, out of the corner of my eye, I've seen them move!"

Ray nearly fell down laughing. "Boo-oo!" he taunted Doug, wriggling his fingers as if invoking a curse. "The scary Victorians are coming after you! Next stop—*The Twilight Zone!*"

"Shut up!" Doug shouted, his anger vanquishing every trace of fear. "Let's go home."

With that, the two inebriated siblings tottered toward downtown Cambridge, Ohio. Snowflakes danced in the beams of the streetlamps and the only sound was the uncoordinated footsteps of Ray and Doug as they trudged through Victorian Village. The mannequin displays, bright with color and alive with Christmas carols during the daytime, appeared that night as dark, shadowy entities, silently waiting.

As the brothers neared the post office, Ray stopped to examine the characters there. The scene depicted a young Victorian lady posting a letter, with her faithful dog at her side.

"Cool!" Ray commented.

"Man, why are we stopping? Hey, don't touch that dog!"

"Chill, Doug. He can't bite. See?"

Ray raised his foot level with the dog's head and delivered a violent kick to the stuffed animal. The dog separated from its stand, the crack of broken boards echoing throughout Wheeling Avenue. As the dog lay on its side, Ray began to laugh. "And one for your mistress, too!" he said, kicking the female mannequin into the mailbox. Doug, seeing the figures broken upon the ground, began to laugh with Ray.

"Why, they're nothing but boards, plaster, and clothes. They don't look spooky at all!"

"Hey, let's see what's on the other side of the street," Ray suggested, grabbing Doug's sleeve.

They half-ran, half-staggered across the slippery street, finding themselves face-to-face with a gaping-mouthed figure wearing a three-cornered hat. Doug leaned forward to read the plaque. "'Town Crier.' I'll give him something to cry about."

He grasped the mannequin's hat, wresting it from the painted head. "Hey, Ray, look!" he blurted, sporting the hat upon his own head. "I'm the town crier! The creepy, spooky town crier!"

"And an ugly one at that," his brother responded.

"What have we here?" asked Doug as he approached another figure. "Check this out—a photographer!"

Doug and Ray circled the platform upon which a Victorian photographer stood behind his ponderous camera. The object of his efforts was a demure woman in a green dress and brown bonnet. "Not bad for plaster and paint," Ray opined , inspecting the female mannequin. "She looks better than most of the chicks at the Blue Jay. I wonder what she'd look like in a bikini?"

"Pretty disgusting, I'd say," Doug answered, "considering there's nothing but boards and nails under those fancy threads."

"I'm going to turn Miss Goody-Two-Shoes into a party girl!" said Ray, reaching into his coat to retrieve a full can of beer.

"Hey, you stole a beer from Tyrone and won't share it with me? I ought to smack you upside the head!"

"Shut up, Doug. The lady needs a beer more than you do."

Ray shoved the can of beer forcibly into the mannequin's lap, ripping its dress. He looked up at the photographer looming above him. "Take a picture of this, Bud!" Ray grunted, thrusting an obscene hand gesture into the figure's face.

"Careful, Ray. That one's stranger than the others."

"There you go again!"

"I'm serious! Look at his eyes—they follow you no matter where you go and they change color. I've looked closely at this guy before. If you stare at him long enough, his skin becomes pinker and his smile gets wider. I'm getting chills up my spine again. Let's get out of here."

"Okay, Scaredy-cat, we'll go."

"Ray, when people see what was done to these mannequins, they're going to be really mad. I read in the newspaper that it takes the artists forty hours just to make the head for one mannequin. I don't want to sit in jail over Christmas."

"Relax, they'll never know who did it. The cops won't even suspect us. Everyone at the Blue Jay knows we always take Turner Avenue home. We're wearing gloves and thick coats with hoods, so no one could identify us, as dark as it is. Besides, no one—not even one car—has been near us since we left the bar."

With their confidence intact, the brothers continued home, looking forward to a long sleep in warm beds.

At nine o'clock the next morning, the men were jolted awake by insistent pounding at their door. "Raymond and Douglas Sowers," bellowed the gruff voice on the other side of the door. "We have a warrant for your arrest."

"I can't believe this!" Ray complained to the officer in the interrogation room. "You can't drag us out of bed and accuse us of vandalism. You have no proof that we did ANYTHING!"

"You're wrong about that," the young officer smirked.

At that moment a suit-clad man carrying a folder entered the room. "Good morning, gentlemen. I'm Detective Pete Lowell."

"Your name will be mud when we sue you!" declared Ray.

"I hope you get a lawyer soon, as you certainly need one," Pete remarked. "And when you do hire one, I wonder what he'll say about these?"

The detective shoved five pictures across the table toward the Sowers brothers. All the pictures were black and white with an amber tint. Ray, who had played with photography as a teenager, recognized them at once as old tintypes, which were in use from the 1860's to the 1920's. He was about to ask why they were brought to the police station to view old photographs when he suddenly gasped. The "old" photographs were of his and Doug's crime spree the previous night.

One by one, Ray and Doug examined each picture with their mouths gaping. There was Ray kicking over the stuffed dog. Another showed Doug ripping the hat from the "Town Crier," and sporting the same hat on his own head in a different photo. The pictures captured every despicable deed, including a close-up of Ray's hand gesture. In each picture the brothers' faces were unmistakable, as if they had willingly posed.

"I didn't want to do it!" blurted Doug. "I told Ray those things give me the creeps and we shouldn't..."

"Shut up!" Ray shouted, causing his brother to burst into tears.

Later that afternoon, the brothers, under the guidance of an attorney, signed confessions and agreed to restitution. Their full punishment would be decided a couple weeks later by a judge.

"That was the fastest confession I've ever seen," Lieutenant Raines commented.

"Me, too," Pete agreed. "It couldn't have happened without those photographs."

"Who gave you those pictures?"

"That's what makes this so strange. When I arrived at work this morning and was told about the damage to the mannequins, my heart sank. I knew that I was in for a grueling investigation and probably still would never catch the lowlifes who did it.

Then, when I went to my office to check my messages, there were the pictures, stacked neatly on my desk. My office was locked—no one could have gotten in there without being seen."

"Sometimes we should simply accept miracles and not question them," the lieutenant muttered between sips of coffee.

As Pete tied up loose ends before leaving work, he spread the tintypes across his desk for one more viewing. The Sowers brothers swore that no one else was on Wheeling Avenue when they engaged in their shenanigans. All the photos appeared to have been taken at close range. Even in a drunken stupor, surely the brothers would have noticed someone lurking near them. Pete was no expert regarding tintypes, but he knew that the flash would have temporarily blinded anyone directly facing the camera. The Sowers' certainly would have remembered such an encounter.

Pete heaved a sigh and leaned back in his chair. "You are an enigma," he addressed the photo in his hand, the most puzzling of all. The image clearly showed Ray Sowers' not-so-pretty face behind an obvious hand gesture. The clarity of the photo suggested the work of a professional; even Ray's chipped incisor was in perfect focus.

Before his attorney advised him to stop speaking to the police, Doug divulged that Ray had directed the gesture toward "the camera guy." *How could that be?* thought Pete. *The photographer scene is much too small for concealing anyone trying to take a furtive picture.* He decided to inspect the tableau on the way home.

Pete parked his car on East Eighth Street and ambled toward the photographer scene. About an inch of snow from the previous night added to the ambience of the Victorian Village. A crowd was already assembling in front of the courthouse for the festive light display. Pete approached the left side of the photographer. The figure was wearing a wine-colored vest, white shirt, and black trousers—*a dapper dresser regardless of the era*, he thought. The photographer's gloved hand was on the camera as he coaxed a smile from his female subject—whose dress remained torn from the indignity of Ray Sowers' intrusion.

Pete turned to face the photographer. A chill climbed his spine. Doug was right! There was something spooky about this mannequin. Pete stared into the painted blue eyes. Wait—did the corners of its mouth just twitch? *You've been working too many hours,* Pete told himself, *and now you're imagining things. But then again, if this mannequin did not take the pictures, who did? Whoever took the close-up of Ray's face had to be standing exactly where the mannequin now stands.*

Pete glanced downward to the base. White plastic, to mimic snow, and an inch of actual snow surrounded the feet of the photographer. If someone had stood in front of the figure, the plastic and snow would have been disturbed.

Pete again looked into the photographer's face. For reasons he would never understand, he placed his hand on the mannequin's shoulder and whispered, "Thank you." He stood silently for a moment with his hand still on the shoulder. Passersby would have thought Pete was part of the tableau. Finally, he turned to walk to his car. He stopped after a few steps to admire the sights before him: Victorian people eagerly awaiting Christmas in a time so far away; children singing along to carols and thrilled with the courthouse light show; strangers greeting each other with a "Merry Christmas."

"I love this time of year," Pete said aloud to himself. A tinny, mechanical voice behind him replied, "So do I. Say 'Cheese!'"

Resting—*The London of Charles Dickens' era was a pedestrian's city. He knew the side streets and alleys well, as did his contemporaries. City dwellers would walk as a primary means of transportation. Benches would have provided a much-needed resting place between stops.*

THE WIDOWS' MIGHT

DICK METHENEY

All their married life, Ray and Mildred Wilson had been big on celebrating Christmas. When their children were little, Ray had dressed up as Santa Claus to hand out the children's presents. The two of them loved the hustle and bustle of the holidays, the sound of friends and neighbors calling out cheerful greetings to each other as they prepared for the coming festivities.

In later years, because their children, Sally and Ray Junior, lived so far away, they had to do their shopping for the children and grandchildren very early in order to get everything wrapped and mailed in time for Christmas. The rest of the year, Ray detested shopping, but he always enjoyed going shopping with Mildred during the holidays.

Junior and his wife were missionaries in the Philippines and, although they were allowed a month's leave every year, they had not been home in ages. Ray had seen their three children only twice in ten years. Both times, he and Mildred had made the exhausting journey to the Philippines to see them. There was always something going on in their busy lives to keep them from making the long trip back to Cambridge.

Sally and her husband were living in Australia, where John worked for an import/export company. They had two children that Ray had never seen other than in photographs. Oh, they sent pictures and a short letter once a month or so, but that was not the same as having them close to you.

That was all behind him now. His beloved wife, Mildred, had passed away last January and things were just not the same. With Mildred gone and his children and grandchildren thousands of miles away, what was there to celebrate? It seemed to him that Christmas was just going to be another lonely day to get through.

In other years, he and Mildred would have begun shopping shortly after Halloween. This year, he could not force himself to get started. He wrote the list, making modifications in it to reflect changes in the grandchildren's ages. He procrastinated, putting off the shopping with a series of flimsy excuses.

This was not like him. All his life Ray had faced everything head on, even Mildred's death. Now, he kept dodging the issue: the weather was too bad, after lunch was soon enough, the stores would be too crowded, or he had other things to do.

Thanksgiving came and went and Ray still had not even started shopping. The morning of December 5th, Ray ran out of excuses. The TV weather lady predicted a high of 62 degrees, sunny and mild. Despondently gathering up his list, wallet, and car keys, he forced himself to drive downtown and search for a parking spot. More than a little surprised to discover there was not a parking place to be found on bustling Wheeling Avenue, he ended up parking on the lower end of Steubenville Avenue.

Still sitting behind the wheel, Ray realized he was not feeling well. *Maybe a touch of the flu,* he thought, *or it might just be another way of trying to get out of doing the shopping. No, I am not going to wuss out this time. This nonsense has gone on long enough. Even if I can finish the shopping today, there will barely be enough time to wrap the presents and get them shipped in time for Christmas.* Resolutely shutting the car door, he started walking south on Sixth Street.

Upon reaching Wheeling Avenue, Ray was feeling a little wobbly on his feet. He managed to make it across the street, feeling damp from a clammy sweat even though the day was reasonably cool. He gratefully sank down on a handy bench.

Clenching his hands on his knees, Ray struggled to control his emotions. After the panic subsided a bit, he looked around with tear-filled eyes. He was seated on a bench in front of Theo's Restaurant and there beside him sat his Mildred. *That is impossible. Mildred is dead. Am I dreaming?* No, he seemed to be awake. *How can this be? Is it really Mildred?* Ray was scrubbing at his tear-filled eyes with his jacket sleeve when he heard a woman's voice say, "Ray? Ray Wilson?"

Averting his eyes from the figure next to him, Ray answered. "Yes. I am Ray Wilson."

"Ray, don't you know me?"

"Of course I remember you. How could I forget my wife…"

"You do remember. Mildred and I were best friends forever. Where have you been hiding? I haven't seen you since Millie's funeral. How are you doing?"

Ray looked past the figure on the bench and recognized Agnes Morefield standing there. *Oh no!* He could not help but feel disappointment. His mind desperately hoped it was Mildred talking to him. Agnes could talk more and faster than most people could listen. Well, maybe that was not all bad; chatting with Agnes would delay the dreaded Christmas shopping.

Ray replied, "Since Mildred's death, I haven't felt like doing much of anything. It about wore me out to deal with the legalities and dispose of her things. I seldom go out of the house except to buy groceries or pay the bills."

Agnes snapped a couple of pictures of him sitting on the bench and asked, "Why not? You are much too young to be a hermit. I read somewhere that hermits lived in caves or on mountaintops. You have a nice little bungalow out in East Pike. You still do live out there, don't you?"

Before Ray could answer, she started talking again. "I certainly didn't become a hermit when Edwin passed. After a suitable mourning time, I decided to be a photographer. A few months of night classes and I got a part-time job with the Jeff."

Ray nodded and said, "So I see. That wouldn't work for me, with my talent for taking pictures. After Mildred's death, I just wanted to be alone." He was hoping Agnes would take the hint and go somewhere else to take her pictures so he could resume his talk with Mildred. No such luck. Agnes kept right on talking.

"Well, you're out and about today, so let's take advantage of the occasion. We are right here in front of Theo's, so let's get a cup of coffee. I'll fill you in on the latest gossip. Do you remember when this place used to be called The Coney Island? It seems like that was only last week."

Before Ray knew it, she had him off the bench and on his way inside, still talking a blue streak. He did not even have a chance to whisper good-bye to Mildred. *Well, a quick cup of coffee could not hurt anything.*

They talked of kids and grandkids. Agnes was appalled that Ray and Mildred's children had not returned to Cambridge when their mother died. She asked, "Neither of them was able to get home for their mother's funeral?"

He shrugged. "It took me a long time to come to grips with that, but Junior and his wife had trekked up into the mountains to conduct a revival and could not be reached for several days. By the time they returned, it was too late to make the trip. Sally had just been operated on for appendicitis and was bedridden. There was no way she could have made the trip. It would have been nice for them to be here, but nothing they could have done would have brought Mildred back."

Agnes snorted and said, "They still should have come, even later on. It would have been a little more considerate."

Ray nodded and said, "It probably would have been that. In my heart, I was grateful not to have to deal with the logistics of two families of virtual strangers descending on me at a time like that. All I wanted to do then was sit in the dark and weep." Wistfully, he continued, "I do wish they could come home this year for Christmas."

Agnes asked, "Did you invite them?"

Ray nodded, "Yeah, I called them Thanksgiving Day. They said they would try, but they've said that before."

Agnes sat there for a minute, then gave him a sheepish grin and said, "I have a plan. You find some excuse to call Sally and Ray Junior and just sort of casually mention you saw a doctor today and then had coffee with a widow woman. That will bring them running home for sure."

Ray protested, "But the part about the doctor would be a lie. That's not a good thing, to lie to them."

Agnes laughed, "But it's not a lie. You see that guy over at that table, the one with the white shirt and tie?"

Ray looked and nodded. "Yes, I see him. So what?"

Agnes said with a giggle, "That is Dan Johnson. He is a pediatrician at the hospital."

Two hours later, filled to overflowing with coffee, they left the restaurant. Ray was dismayed to find two strangers sitting on the bench next to his Mildred. Agnes whipped out her camera and began snapping pictures of them. She told Ray, "It looks like you lost your seat." Ray nodded and said, "Well, Agnes, it has been nice talking to you. I had better get my errands done before it gets too late."

He walked east on Wheeling Avenue, looking in the store windows as he went. He thought he could still hear Agnes two blocks away, but maybe it was just his ears ringing from all her chatter over coffee. His list had nine names on it and he had better get to shopping if he was going to get it completed.

It was nearly 1 p.m. when Ray decided to walk back to his car and maybe on the way check to see if Agnes had left her post in front of Theo's. He desperately wanted to sit on that bench and see if his Mildred would talk to him. It was risky, because if Agnes saw him she would drag him into the restaurant for lunch and another two hours of gossip. His best bet would be to cut down Tenth Street and then take a left on Steubenville to where he had parked his car.

His armful of parcels safely stashed in his trunk, Ray cautiously approached Wheeling Avenue and paused to peer around the corner for Agnes. Good, she was nowhere to be seen. Hurrying across the street, he quickly seated himself on the bench next to the same lady and immediately realized it was one of the Dickens mannequins. *How could I be so dense?*

Feeling like a dunce, Ray was getting to his feet when Flossie Bergholtz came out of the restaurant and nearly bumped into him. Well, she *had* been a Bergholtz back when they were going to school. After graduation, Flossie had married Dan Rickover and moved away from Cambridge. He had not seen her in all these years. There was a handsome, much younger man with her.

Flossie said, "Ray? Ray Wilson? I bet you don't remember me."

Ray gave her a sheepish grin and said, "Of course I remember you, Flossie. We were in the same class at school. You married Dan and moved away. I didn't know you were back in town."

Flossie said, "I have been here for a couple of weeks. I was sorry to hear about Mildred. I know how hard it is to lose someone you love. Dan died last Christmas. This is my youngest son, Michael. Mike, this is Ray Wilson. We went to school together. He was my secret heartthrob back in the seventh grade, but he only had eyes for Mildred Pauley even back then."

They all laughed and Ray said, "Don't let her fool you, Michael. She was a cheerleader and runner-up for homecoming queen. I would be willing to bet she couldn't even see me for the football players drooling over her."

Flossie laughed, "Oh yes, braces, glasses, freckles, and all."

They agreed to get together soon and reminisce some more. Although Ray only had about half of his shopping done, he decided to call it a day. As he started walking back toward his car, a feeling of guilt washed over him for having enjoyed himself talking to Flossie and her son. *I'm sorry Mildred. For a few minutes there, I forgot to be lonely.*

As Ray wrapped Christmas presents that afternoon, Agnes' words kept running through his mind. *"You find some excuse to call Sally and Ray Junior and just sort of casually mention you saw a doctor today and had coffee with a widow woman. That'll bring them running home for sure."* While that would not be an outright lie, it was getting very close.

There was quite a difference in seeing a doctor across a busy restaurant and going to the doctor's office. But not any worse than the kids saying they would try to come home for the holidays and then not coming. For all her gift of gab, maybe Agnes did have a workable plan. He felt one corner of his mouth turn up in a little grin. Actually, he had had coffee with one widow and talked for several minutes with another. *Would that make up for stretching the story about the doctor? Maybe.*

He sure would like to see his kids and grandkids, especially at Christmas. Should he call Sally or Junior first? What would they think about him calling just to talk? You couldn't just blurt out the part about the doctor and the widow women. Ray would have to be very subtle about this thing if he was going to make it work. With the difference in time zones, timing would be important. *Call too early and no one will be home, too late and everyone will be in bed.*

First thing in the morning would be the best; it would be evening over there, after dinner and before the kids went to sleep. As the television blabbed its way through the evening news and weather, Ray went over what he wanted to say and just how to say it. For the first time in ten and a half months, Ray did not shed tears before falling asleep.

After drinking a whole pot of high-test coffee, Ray got up the nerve to make his phone calls. He had decided on calling Sally first. They chatted for several minutes about how everyone was doing before he casually mentioned having coffee with Agnes Morefield. Ray told Sally, "Agnes' husband passed away two years ago. She talked for nearly two hours over coffee at Theo's yesterday. Sometimes that woman can talk faster than I can listen." Ray repeated his invitation for Sally and her family to come for a visit for the holidays.

Before they hung up, she gave him her standard answer, "It would be nice to get away from the summer heat for a while, but I'll have to check with John to see if he can get away that long."

Ray disconnected and quickly dialed Junior's number. He wanted to get his spiel in before Sally could get on the phone and tell her brother about his having coffee with Agnes. Luck or fate must have been on his side, Junior picked up the phone on the second ring—any other time one of the grandkids would get to the phone first.

Beginning the call with the usual banal talk of the weather and how the grandkids were doing in school was all right with Ray. It gave him a chance to work up his courage. When the conversation lagged, Ray casually mentioned, "I ran into Flossie Bergholtz while I was Christmas shopping the other day. I haven't seen her since we graduated high school. She certainly has aged well. Her son, Mike, was with her. He seemed like a nice young man."

Junior asked, "Are you doing all right, Dad?"

Ray said, "Well, I was feeling a little poorly for a while, but since I saw the doctor I feel much better. Is there any chance you guys can get home for Christmas?"

"I don't think we can this year, maybe next year. Things are kind of hectic here right now. I'll call you if anything changes."

Ray answered, "Well, I sure would like to have all of our family together for the holidays. If I feel up to it, I'll come out to see you next Christmas." He felt there was just the right emphasis on these words to get his point across. After getting through the goodbyes and hanging up the phone, he felt just a little guilty for the deception he had used on his own children.

Ray hurried through his meager breakfast and got dressed. He had to get moving if he was going to get the decorations up from the basement and find the tree stand before hotfooting it down to Theo's in time for Agnes's coffee break. Maybe, if the weather was nice, he would sit on the bench out in front for a while. You never knew when another widow might walk past.

Father Christmas Comes to Cambridge— *Father Christmas typified the spirit of good cheer at Christmas, and was reflected in the "Ghost of Christmas Present" in Dickens' 'A Christmas Carol.' He was normally portrayed as a plump, bearded man dressed in a long green fur-lined robe. This mannequin's face is that of Grant Hafley of AVC Communications, mastermind behind the Guernsey County Courthouse Holiday Light Show.*

THE SECRET OF FATHER CHRISTMAS

MARTHA JAMAIL

"**H**ello, there! Yes, I'm speaking to you. Look up here. I am the figure in the green robe trimmed in white. A crown of evergreens is around my head and I carry a staff and lantern to guide me on my journey. My name is Father Christmas.

"My friends and I stand along this street to welcome you to Dickens Victorian Village in our town of Cambridge, Ohio. Though I stand before you frozen in time, I can still see you and want to wish you and your family a very Merry Christmas. I also have something very important to tell you.

"I am also known as the 'Spirit of Christmas Present,' created from the imagination of the famous writer, Charles Dickens. I was the second spirit called upon to visit Ebenezer Scrooge in the story *A Christmas Carol*.

"There were three of us, all spirit visitors, who were called upon to impress Mr. Scrooge to change his life. Oh, he was a wealthy man, that one. Scrooge possessed great riches and he guarded them very well. He not only denied his faithful servant, Bob Cratchit, fair wages for his work, he also stingily rationed him the bits of coal needed to keep his workplace warm. Rarely did poor Bob Cratchit remove his gloves and comforter while at work. Old Man Scrooge kept his heart, as well as his fortune, under lock and key.

"Oh, Ebenezer doubted the spirits when we appeared to him that fateful Christmas Eve. At first, he even blamed our late night visits on indigestion or possibly eating something that was spoiled. Thankfully, he listened to our message of the great joy in sharing with those less fortunate than ourselves, and soon he believed. Why, the very next morning Scrooge was able to change his life completely.

"The story *A Christmas Carol* was so popular it spread from England throughout the world, and I became the model for your Americanized version of Father Christmas. You Americans call him Santa Claus. Do you know why?

"Well, you see, even further back in history, the character of Father Christmas was based on an actual person who lived in the 4th Century. His name was Nicholas. He was known throughout Europe for possessing a great and generous spirit, and was a champion of children. In what some considered medieval legend and folklore, Nicholas even performed miracles on suffering children, thus earning him the title of Saint before his name. The Dutch variant of the name St. Nicholas is Santa Claus.

"What? You don't believe in Santa? Well, you should. Santa means "saint" and who wouldn't want to believe that a person possessing the qualities of a saint actually does exist? One dictionary definition of a saint is a virtuous person, a very kind and unselfish person. And I'm sure you know a few people that could fit that description.

"As a child, I'm sure you can remember the joy and wonder of waking up early on Christmas morning and seeing the magical glow of lights reflected on the presents Santa had left under the tree. It didn't have to happen every Christmas, but, if you were lucky, just once was enough to fix the moment forever in your memory.

"Then, as an adult, you want to replicate that moment again and again for other children. It could be for your own children, or even someone else's child. You see, that moment of joy and wonder is so much more than just the presents under the tree. It also nurtures in us a belief in something bigger than ourselves, that sense of the awesome power of goodness and love. Santa is the "spirit of generosity" that lives in all of us.

"So there you have my secret. YOU are Santa. Don't you believe in yourself?"

⁂

"It is a fair, even-handed, noble adjustment of things, that while there is infection in disease and sorrow, there is nothing in the world so irresistibly contagious as laughter and good humour."

~ Charles Dickens, *A Christmas Carol*.

The Sled Maker—*"Christmas is a day of meaning and traditions, a special day spent in the warm circle of family and friends."—Margaret Thatcher*

FINDING ROSEBUD

RICK BOOTH

Driving down the Pacific Coast Highway towards Scott Creek, a dozen thoughts fought for my attention in anticipation of what I might find at the old family home there—treasure, cobwebs, or perhaps, in a strange metaphorical way, a child's sled named Rosebud. The air was clear and warm as a breeze came off the water. As always, when adapting East Coast eyes to the West after a long flight, there suddenly seemed to be more sun and sky than earth's geometry should properly allow. In California, too, the rental cars seem almost tree-huggingly embarrassed to be running on gasoline instead of, say, solar. It always takes a while to adapt to the West. And still, throughout the drive, the ending of the old movie Citizen Kane kept running through my mind.

Cousin Jan Gibson and I, the closest living relatives to our grandfather, Theodore C. Monrow, had agreed to meet at the old family Scott Creek home to assess, divide, and dispose of the estate Grandfather left behind. The house itself was a museum piece—part castle, part palace, and part Western range manor in the style of the Cartwright's Ponderosa on old Bonanza reruns— the kind of structure that's obviously built by someone with too little architectural sense and too much money. Originally constructed in 1872, the house was added onto in dribs and drabs through the 1920's. We in the family often wondered if William Randolph Hearst's sprawling San Simeon castle on down the coast might have been inspired by great-great-great-grandfather Monrow's hilltop statement of local hegemony. Bought and paid for with second-hand Gold Rush money, the original grounds had been nearly a square mile in size, more recently diminished to just the eighty immediate acres at the top of a coastal range hill, enough to always ensure an unobstructed view of Pacific sunsets in the ocean two miles away.

Grandfather, though kind and generous to kin, had always been somewhat the family recluse, and even more so since Grandma died in 1998. He had done his part to keep the family assets relatively intact despite the fact that he'd lived to be 97, with some not inconsiderable medical and home care expenses in his last fifteen years. He'd once owned and managed three restaurants in San Jose and Cupertino. The area later was better known as Silicon Valley. Land prices spiraled and left him with a healthy nest egg when he retired and sold the businesses in '87.

His death, though not entirely unexpected, caught both Jan and me by surprise on the day that, by chance, he didn't wake up. The morning home attendant found him and notified the family. The funeral, five days after he died, was my first reunion with Jan in more than a decade, though we'd kept in touch by phone and e-mail on a tenuous cousinly basis through the years. Jan had settled in Evanston, Illinois, and I in a suburb of Philadelphia. We'd had two months to prepare for and plan this second joint trip to the San Francisco area to divide up and dispose of the estate. The Anderson Estate Liquidation Service had finished the first part of its job, sorting and organizing the home's contents for auction. Now it was just up to Jan and me to review the items, take what we wanted, and green-light the sale to proceed.

Jan was already there when I arrived. The oversized Stetson on her head immediately bespoke that she'd already found a keepsake memento. We both had childhood memories of Grandfather in cowboy hats and boots at family reunions and the summer weeks we sometime spent with Grandma and him in the early 1960's. The smile coming out from under the hat, though, was inimitably Jan's. That part hadn't changed in 50 years.

"Well, have you found the treasure of the Sierra Madre here yet?"I greeted Jan with my own returning grin. We both had had the slightly fanciful wish that a secret cache of gold, left over from the days of the forty-niners, or some other such long-forgotten family treasure, might come to light in the inventory. There was no such luck though, as Jan reported her preliminary findings to me from under that nostalgic headpiece. Entering the house past the junk pile deposited in the garage area for removal, it soon became clear that the Anderson Company had done a good job of organizing the assets. Both Jan and I had homes of our own which had become rather full through the process of raising families, so the decision was made to part with all but the most economically small and memorable keepsakes still left in the home for us to divide. Shoeboxes of hundred-year-old letters, of course, were to be kept for historical inspection, but the hundred-year-old riding saddles would go off to deep-pocketed collectors with more appreciation for them than either Jan or I would give them. Sold, they would perhaps live to ride again, receiving far more appreciation and better fates than to molder in humid basements east of the Mississippi. I kept the World War II service medals, and Jan the ones from Korea.

As we exited the home the same way we came in, Jan commented in passing by the junk pile, "I guess this is the stuff that's not worth two cents." I knew exactly what she meant, of course, because that was Grandpa's usual way of expressing disdain for anything. The phrase had stuck with both our parents too, and been ingrained in each of us as well. All of us Monrow descendants knew we'd better grow up to be worth at least "two cents," or we'd be in trouble. And so the two of us stood in the driveway for quite some time, reminiscing about former days at the family home, about parents and grandparents, and the rather enduring mystery of the progenitor of our line, a man named Richard Monrow, who came out of Genealogical Nowhere to found the small family dynasty there in an era of gold fever and an age of hope and glory.

As Jan and I were finally about to part ways in the driveway, my eyes came to rest on that beautiful estate-front view of the distant calm Pacific, and the haunting thoughts of Citizen Kane returned. The movie, of course, ended with the supreme irony that an old child's sled named Rosebud—the key to a running, unsolved mystery throughout the film regarding the last words of a newspaper dynasty's founder—is thoughtlessly consigned to the incinerator without concern or notice. The urge to recheck the refuse heap drew me back. Not wanting to delay Jan further, I bid her farewell with best regards to her husband and sons. Back at the refuse heap in the otherwise empty garage, I picked through damaged lamps and furniture, stacks of thirty- and forty-year-old magazines, and dusty boxes of old utility bills for perhaps fifteen minutes before coming upon a small, exceedingly dirty wooden crate which at first glance appeared to be empty. A closer look revealed a book, somewhat tall and wide and moderately thin, yet so covered in the airborne grime of years that it matched the tone of the bottom of the crate. This I extracted, first blowing as much dust off the top as my lungs could muster, and then wiping it over with a paper towel for good measure. After a thorough hand washing, I settled into the soon-to-be-auctioned porch glider to study my find in the sun.

It was clear there was writing on the book's cover, but it was nearly indecipherable, having merged with the embedded dust. When opened though, the pages came easily to life, having yellowed only a little with the passage of time. Dated 1858 and published in London, it was a brief, bound collection of short stories by Charles Dickens—*The Poor Traveller*, *Boots at the Holly-Tree Inn*, and *Mrs. Gamp*, to name a few. Turning the pages one by one, old illustrations and stories came to life. At the start of *The Boots at the Holly Tree Inn* though, three separate frail documents were inserted. Carefully separating them so as to avoid unnecessary flaking or cracking, I recognized the first two by their jagged cut edges as ancient indentured contracts.

The first indentured contract, a hugely exciting find, was for the seven-year wheelwright apprenticeship of my great-great-great-grandfather, Richard Monrow, in 1842 to a master craftsman named John Goss at a place called Washington, Ohio. Later research showed the modern name of the place to be Old Washington, Ohio, today. This was the man who built the very house I sat in with the fortune made sutling to the gold miners! But how did a young wheelwright, sworn to serve an apprenticeship through 1849, find his way to California?

The second document only deepened the mystery. This was another indenture, but not for apprenticeship. To pay a debt, the parents of 13-year-old Mary Ann Strowd in 1845 had bound over their daughter to serve the family of Isaac McKay for five years in a southeastern Indiana county by the Ohio River. Recalling that all we knew of Richard Monrow's wife was her first name, Mary, I wondered if I'd hit more family history gold. Could Miss Strowd have become his wife?

The third document, a long handwritten tract, explained the other two. My hands nearly shook as I read it:

"Upon the death of my beloved wife, Mary, December 29, 1899, I, Richard Monrow, here set down our story. I was born in Bristol, England, in 1826, the son of Robert and Phillipa Monrow who came to these United States in 1835, settling at St. Clairsville, Ohio, to farm. To provide for my future, in 1842 I was indented in wheel making, it being a profitable trade on the National Road in those years, to Mr. Goss of near the town of Washington, thirty miles west. When Mr. Goss fell ill in 1846 and could not provide sufficient food for his family and for me, least of all, I took liberty to remove myself west with the National Road, wagons and coaches always being in need of wheelwrights. It is my belief Mr. Goss agreed with my decision, for it was told me by travelers he offered that year only a penny for my return. In 1847, I resided near Cincinnati, where I found employ in the building of steamboats. The next year, at market, I met Mary Ann Strowd who was quite young and also an indentured runaway from home service west of Cincinnati. In furtherance of her escape and my work, we determined to reach St. Louis by river, she hiring to cook and I to attend to the boat's carpentry. Again, word followed us that Mary was not wanted back, another poor penny reward being offered for her return. Wheelwright work in Missouri was plentiful, as so many pioneers were beginning to go west. When word of gold in California came, I determined to go there, as did Mary, I being a wagon train's wheelwright and Mary a widower's helper to mind his small children. At San Francisco, the demand for wagons being great and my resources being few, I set about the making of wheels for prices triple again what I ever had sold before, the need for them accounting for their price. With Mary's help at bookkeeping, the extra money we

had we used to contract for shipped supplies and miners'
goods. Few of the miners found riches, but they all left their
coins at my business. This is how I became a wealthy sutler
instead of an empty-pocketed miner. Mary and I were
married in 1850. We had three sons, Joseph C., William C.,
and James C., all with middle name Charles in honor of Mr.
Charles Dickens whose stories of hardships, runaways, and
good fortune inspired us through the years and entertained
our children on many a long ago day. Mary's favorite story
was Boots at the Holly-Tree Inn, which some also call The
Runaway Couple, it being the story of two young runaways
who set off to be married. And so I leave this writing, in
memory of Mary, my good wife for nigh on fifty years, to
mark the story she so liked and which so reminded her of
ourselves. I had not thought of those penny rewards that she
and I were said to be worth until I saw the two pennies on her
eyes in death and thought maybe I was seeing a sign—two
pennies to bring us back home."

The note was signed "Richard Monrow," but some of the ink
had been smeared at spots, as if by drops of water. Those, no
doubt, were from tears. It was all I could do to avoid adding
drops of my own as well.

Though it had only been half an hour since Jan had left, it
seemed ages as my mind floated in reverie for ancestors and
ancient family traditions. I, Richard Charles Monrow, had never
known quite why it was told me that all Monrow men should be
given the middle name Charles. It was just an expected tradition,
one I never thought to question. In our family, too, the slightly
idiosyncratic phrase "not worth two cents," used to disparage
someone or something, took on a faint echo of history in my
mind. So too, the annual family readings of *A Christmas Carol*

when I was a child—perhaps a remnant of days past and the flight to California and fortune.

As I closed up the book, its document treasures resealed inside, I thought once again with gratitude of the movie Citizen Kane and its nudge of recollection to look back one last time in search of some long-forgotten, personal memory. It mattered little that I'd not found Granddad's hidden treasure of the Sierra Madre, or even a modest stash of old cash and coin. Turning to lock the screened porch door behind me, the book in my hand tilted vertical. Suddenly, with a jangling ring, I heard something hit the pavement. There on the stones by the front steps of old Richard Monrow's hilltop house lay two fine pennies each far more than a century old, fallen out from behind the backmost pages. Picking them up, I slipped them back inside the book.

The breeze blew gently as the sun sank lower in the sky. Looking first at the book and then out at the soft, blue ocean, a smile welled up in me from that place in spirit or mind where symmetry and perfect days are most cherished. A word in the wind broke the silence. For reasons too deep to recall, I whispered "Rosebud."

Author's Note: The preceding story was inspired by two actual notices published in the 1840's regarding runaways. When an indentured servant or apprentice would run away in breach of contract, the master of said servant or apprentice was generally required to post a notice of reward for their return. Those who, in fact, were not wanted back would be advertised with one cent rewards to help prevent their return.

The following advertisement for the return of runaway apprentice Richard Monrow was first advertised in the Guernsey

Jeffersonian, published in Old Washington, Ohio, on April 9, 1846:

ONE CENT REWARD

RAN away from the subscriber on the 1st day of February 1846, Richard Monrow an indented apprentice. He is about 19 years of age, of a small size, is somewhat cross-eyed, and of a down, saucy countenance. He had on when he left a fur cap, an old jeans coat, and brown colored pants with some patches on them. All persons are hereby warned from harboring or trusting said boy on my account. Any person returning said apprentice shall receive the above reward and no thanks. JOHN W. GOSS.

Two years later, the following advertisement was run in the Vevay Campaign Palladium newspaper of southeastern Indiana on August 12, 1848, for the return of indentured servant Mary Ann Strowd:

One Cent Reward.

RAN AWAY from the subscriber, living in Craig township, Switzerland county, Indiana, on the 3d day of August, 1848, a bound girl named Mary Ann Strowd, between 15 and 16 years of age. All persons are hereby forbid harboring this girl under the penalty of Law. The above reward will be paid for the return of said girl, and no thanks. ISAAC McKAY.

Both Richard Monrow and Mary Ann Strowd disappeared from traceable historic records after their escapes. In the spirit of a happily resolved Dickensian tale, I wished to discover that they each might have found in life their own happy ending, perhaps even together. I hope they did.

The Fezziwig Ball—*"Christmas is a day of meaning and traditions, a special day spent in the warm circle of family and friends."*— Margaret Thatcher

THE FEZZIWIG CHALLENGE

BEVERLY WENCEK KERR

"**B**et by Christmas you won't fit into the Victorian dress you bought last year to volunteer at Ye Olde Curiosity Shoppe. We both gained weight during the winter. I'll bet you a hundred dollars you won't be able to wear it," smirked Ralph. Since Dickens Victorian Village wasn't his cup of tea, he couldn't figure out its attraction for his wife, Elizabeth.

"Hmm, a hundred dollars? I wouldn't mind making a bet, but let's make it a little more interesting. Instead of a hundred dollars, if I fit into my Victorian gown," challenged Elizabeth, "you will accompany me to Mr. Fezziwig's Ball. If not, then you can journey to Alaska on that black bear hunting trip you've been talking about."

"Yeah sure, Elizabeth. There's no way you'll fit in that dress!" Ralph laughed as he drew a mental picture. "I'm going to get my hunting gear ready for Alaska." Leaving the room with a big smile on his face, Ralph whistled the song, *North to Alaska*.

It was only June, so Elizabeth had a few months to shed those unwanted pounds. The beautiful lacy gown buttoned up the front with tiny pearl buttons, but a two-inch gap at the waistline became the biggest problem. She needed to do some new exercises, as well as cut back on food portions.

Reading *The Daily Jeffersonian* later that evening, Elizabeth spotted an article which sparked her interest. Dickens Universal, located in an old Universal Pottery building, was asking for volunteers to help prepare the mannequins before they were placed on the streets in November. Helping with the mannequins sounded intriguing, and possibly would be valuable exercise to help her fit in that beautiful Victorian gown.

When Elizabeth walked through the doors of Dickens Universal on their next work day, a busy scene met her eyes. Immediately, Cindy, Sharon, and Lindy, the Restoration Team organizers, explained the work of various volunteers. Walking briskly down the rows of characters, they would call out suggestions to the other volunteers—"The bobby needs a new hat...That school child's scarf looks a bit ragged...Don't forget to vacuum her skirt...Wash Scrooge's face." No one loafed because there was an abundance of work to be completed in order for all the scenes to be refurbished before November.

Elizabeth was immediately put to work. Before long she was vacuuming dust off mannequins, polishing shoes, and replacing clothing as needed. Sometimes it felt like a sweat tank down there, but she enjoyed all the people who worked on the restoration. This friendly bunch of volunteers almost felt like family.

On their next work day, Elizabeth mentioned that she was sewing some curtains at home. The organizers, desperately needing people who could make new costumes and fix old ones, were excited. Now she was repairing torn skirts and coats, plus tacking down the mannequins' clothes so they wouldn't blow off in the wind.

In August, Elizabeth decided to try on her Victorian gown. Just another inch and it would fasten! Her heart beat fast in anticipation of the ball, but she didn't say anything to Ralph.

He was in the garage, getting his hunting equipment cleaned

and ready for Alaska. Even though the black bear hunt would not begin until early spring, he was already assembling things he would need. Binoculars were important for spotting a bear, therefore, he had recently received in the mail the latest Pentax DCF model with the largest field of view available. A waterproof coat and boots could prove extremely important—you never know what the weather is going to be like in Alaska. It can change on the spur of the moment, but he was already used to that in Ohio.

Elizabeth enjoyed her work so much that one evening she placed a mannequin in her front seat to take home with her, so she could fix its costume during the week. When she pulled into the drive, Ralph shook his head. "Have you lost your mind? People will think you're crazy, driving around with a mannequin in your car!"

"You know, Ralph, after a while you begin to think of these characters as real people. They seem to take on a life all their own. So tonight I brought Samantha home with me so I can fix her dress and shoes a little better." Elizabeth was so busy with her newfound enjoyment, evening snacks didn't even cross her mind.

Ralph began to worry about that bet. Elizabeth did appear to be losing a few pounds with all those hot days down at Dickens Universal. "You've been so busy. Let's go out to dinner tonight," suggested Ralph one summer evening while whistling his favorite song these days, *North to Alaska*. Elizabeth was quite surprised. Ralph seldom mentioned the possibility of an evening out together. Could he be trying to sabotage her weight loss? If so, she'd fool him by eating very sensibly.

"Let's head downtown to Theo's. We can have a piece of their delicious pie for dessert," Ralph continued. Now Elizabeth felt almost certain that her reasoning was correct. But it still would be relaxing to enjoy a delicious dinner without having to cook it herself.

That evening, Samantha was left propped up in a lawn chair on the back patio, where Elizabeth had been repairing the mannequin's Victorian shoes. Ralph and Elizabeth bantered back and forth about their bet until they found a parking place downtown. Walking into Theo's with her husband for an evening on the town, Elizabeth's face shone like a gold coin after being polished by Scrooge.

During dinner, a storm blew into the area with some high winds. Samantha crossed Elizabeth's mind, but she was relieved to remember that the mannequins were accustomed to being outside in the cold, blowing snow. This shouldn't be a problem.

But, back home, the wind blew Samantha into the yard, where she lay looking rather forlorn. Through the torrential rain, a nearby neighbor could see someone in the yard, not moving a muscle. Immediately, thinking it was Elizabeth, she quickly called 911.

Shortly, Ralph and Elizabeth arrived back home. Imagine their surprise when they found an ambulance, a police car, and several neighbors in their yard.

"What happened?" asked Elizabeth, out of breath after running around the house. "Who got hurt here?"

Blushing as red as the ambulance lights, the neighbor explained what had happened. "I'm very glad to see it wasn't you out here, Elizabeth. What is that Dickens character doing at your place anyway?"

"Oh, I'm helping this year with refurbishing the characters," explained the surprised volunteer. "I had no idea the wind would kick up like that. I was trying to dry the glue I used to fix her shoes."

Ralph rolled his eyes and threw up his arms. "You never know what Elizabeth is going to do these days. This Dickens Victorian Village has really gotten under her skin."

As the days rolled on, Ralph checked online for hunting facilities in Alaska, while Elizabeth did some extra side bends. Elizabeth was wise enough not to mention the Fezziwig Ball to Ralph, but it remained in the back of her mind all of the time.

November finally rolled around, with the ball only a couple weeks away. Elizabeth had been trying her dress on every week. Now it was even a little loose around the waist. Buttoning it was not difficult any longer. She would definitely be ready for the ball.

She waited until a few days before the big event to waltz into the living room, spinning gracefully in the beautiful blue satin gown with white roses around the hemline and on the sleeves. Ralph's jaw fell as she floated through the room. He'd lost the bet and his trip to Alaska. *But my*, he thought, *Elizabeth does look lovely in that gown.*

"Yes, Ralph, we are going to Mr. Fezziwig's Ball this weekend," said Elizabeth with a glow on her face. She twirled round and round, as excited as Bob Cratchit with a pay raise.

The evening finally arrived and Ralph proudly put his arm around Elizabeth's waist before entering the ballroom. "You look absolutely fantastic," he told Elizabeth. "I'm so proud of you for helping with Dickens Victorian Village...and fitting into that gorgeous gown so beautifully."

The room glowed in the light from the oil lamps and a blazing fireplace, which also made the ladies' jewels glitter. Displaying all the colors of the rainbow, their exquisite gowns were trimmed with ribbons and lace as well as the sparkling jewels. Groups of balloons, a popular decoration at Charles Dickens' parties, added color and gaiety to the ceiling. Beautifully decorated trees made the ballroom appear to be a Wonderland. The atmosphere was filled with the spirit of Christmas.

Violinists strolled through the crowd, playing songs from ages gone by. Once in a while, voices were raised in song. Mr. Fezziwig's voice greeted everyone with, "Hilli-Ho, let's dance up a storm." Women in their fanciest gowns and men in their coattails filled the room with high-spirited enjoyment as they joined the dancers. These couples, in the words of Charles Dickens, were "people who were not to be trifled with; people who would dance and had no notion of walking."

When the fiddler struck up *Sir Roger de Coverley*, an English version of the Virginia Reel, merriment flowed throughout the dance floor. Gentlemen bowed elegantly and ladies swished their dresses as they moved quickly around the floor, changing partners in one of the traditional set dances.

Elizabeth reached over and grasped Ralph's hand, pulling him gently. "Let's dance like we did years ago at the Cambridge City Park pavilion in the summertime. Remember how much fun we had there with our friends?"

"Ah, Liz, that was long ago. I don't even remember how to dance. Let's just watch."

"Dancing, Ralph, is like riding a bicycle. Once you know how to do it, you always remember. Please, give it a try."

"Probably better or I'll never hear the end of this," grumbled Ralph under his breath as they headed to the dance floor.

A beautiful old waltz played as Elizabeth almost floated, while Ralph plodded, to join the other dancers. Ralph reluctantly took hold of Elizabeth as best he could remember. After a few measures, they were gliding over the dance floor quite smoothly. As she spun around, Elizabeth noticed something interesting about some of the others on the floor.

As the music changed to a promenade, Charles Dickens and his wife walked arm in arm while Prince William spun Kate around gracefully. Scrooge scowled at all the happy frolicking, but suddenly his usually stormy eyes filled with tears as he remembered Belle, his beautiful lady of long ago, who left him because he was too interested in money.

Elizabeth couldn't believe her eyes! Why, they looked just like the mannequins she had been working with at Dickens Universal…but they were standing now on the downtown streets of Cambridge for Dickens Victorian Village, weren't they? Could it be? Were they really here dancing or was it just a figment of her imagination? As they floated among all the Dickens characters, Elizabeth felt right at home, as if she were at a dance with her best friends.

Ralph looked lovingly at Elizabeth and said, "I had forgotten how much fun we used to have dancing. We're going to have to do this more often."

"Ralph, this is the happiest time I've had in ages. Thanks for coming and dancing this evening. This is the best early Christmas present I ever had. Maybe we will find a way for you to take that black bear adventure."

Ralph attempted to hide his smile. His reservations were already completed!

Tiny Tim and Bob Cratchit—*Charles Dickens wrote "A Christmas Carol" in roughly six weeks. The Cratchit family was based on his own childhood life, he being the eldest of five siblings. Tiny Tim was representative of all children living in poverty.*

BIG MAN IN TIGHT SKIN

DWAIN WILLIAMS

He was anything but tiny while hobbling around the old house with a crutch and a smile. Deep appreciation for those who cared for his ailments soothed a young heart with such beat for life and limited time to prove worthiness.

The years had not been kind to his frail frame, but life's struggles had not dulled a precious spirit instilled within. Watching and listening to the songbirds of summer brought such peace. He could rub the underside of the sore crutch arm while nestling into the rickety wooden chair. Elbows resting upon the window sill, a mind drifted off to sleep, dreaming of his favorite season…winter…

Oh, what sounds the gently falling snowflakes made, but he had to listen closely. The aroma of a slow-roasting goose and what trimmings Mom could afford tickled the taste buds. He heard Daddy's footsteps on the squeaky wooden floor and felt those loving hands touch his shoulders. "Tim, Christmas dinner is ready."

All senses touched, he awoke from the joyous dream realizing time could be short if God called. Clasping the short crutch, he knew the walk well. He glanced upward, giving words of thanks to God for the chance to grow tall and strong enough to repair the cracked ceiling. "I'll reach you and then some," as a tear of pain slowly came. "Why can't life be simple for those holding hope for a gifted tomorrow?" The ceiling answered, to his astonishment. "Hold on to both crutches; you are walking for two." Confused, he glanced at his single crutch. Again, loudly: "You're mending a soul, and the crutch of another."

Completely baffled, Tim pivoted around the doorjamb, headed down a long hallway toward whatever the day might bring. Strange thoughts had been whirling through his young mind, and sorting dream from reality was not easy, but the recognizable tone of Scrooge's voice was not to be mistaken as he entered the sparsely furnished sitting room.

"Must you make such noise with that stick?" he said sharply.

"I wish to someday not require its services," was Tim's gentle reply. And with that, Scrooge slammed the one-hinged wooden door shut while cursing the day in general.

"Daddy, why does God permit such bitter souls to dwell in the hearts of some?" he asked.

"There are those of the world who create problems for those who wish to solve them; the remainder simply don't care," came Mr. Cratchit's reply.

Puzzled by his daddy's answer, Tim glanced upward in a manly way. "Lord, I wish to be a solver, not a creator of all, as You are." Once again, Tim glanced at flaws in the architecture and thought to himself, *If only Mr. Scrooge would supply the materials, I could make this a home Mom could be proud of...at least the parts I can reach.*

Pogo-ing back down the hallway, he studied the squeaky floor, looking for a starting point if the goal became reality. "I know the floor will always be within reach," he said quietly. As the months passed, ceiling and floor spoke often, and it was not uncommon for the walls to chime in. "I wish Mr. Scrooge understood that my crutch was not meant to step in the way of good intentions," Tim murmured one night. He heard the soft words, "Be patient," and drifted into a peaceful slumber.

The next morning brought quite a surprise as sunlight enhanced the cracked kitchen windowpane. Upon the table lay a new hammer and a poke of nails. "Where did these come from?" he quizzed himself. There was no answer this time. Hesitantly, Tim crutched backward, fearful of uncertainty.

Gathering his thoughts, he rested his bony elbows on the windowsill, palms clasped around his pale thin face. "Lord, I'm not sure what's going on, but knowing you have a hand in it sets my heart to a comfortable beat."

Instantly the ceiling spoke, "Mr. Scrooge wants you to have the tools of life, one by one. He simply has trouble organizing his toolbox for you."

Eleven days until Christmas, the songbirds had long since vanished in search of their own comfortable corner of the round world. Tim understood the simplicity and complexity of nature in spite of being housebound for the majority of his short life.

Not knowing that time can change certain things, he pondered how best to use the gift of nails. Leaping into his memory bank, Tim remembered Mom saying, "Those loose boards will someday cause a fall worthy of a splint."

"I'll start on the porch," he calmly uttered as someone inside him reacted, "no matter how cold it is. A coat will cut the wind."

His coat did indeed scare away the cold wind, but not the numb fingers and blackened thumbnail, which concerned his observing Mom deeply.

"I want to have this buttoned up before Daddy gets home. I don't want him to trip and fall after a long day's work. He gives us so much through his efforts for Mr. Scrooge." Those teeth-chattering words struck Mom to the bone.

Worn from toil but bent on completion, Tim crutched through the kitchen door satisfied with what was accomplished. The smell of stew boosted an energy level unknown to his tiny appetite as he slid softly into a kitchen chair of questionable integrity. Thinking well beyond his years, he asked, "Mom, is it a waste of time to plan for the future?"

"Oh, heavens no," she said stoutly. "Your future is just beginning. You and Mr. Scrooge!"

"Do you think Daddy will notice?" She smiled in a motherly way, the only answer needed. Talking with Daddy as the heartwarming stew was consumed by all, Tim thought, *Maybe Daddy didn't notice my work through night's cold and darkness.*

"Tim, I'll tuck you in when you're ready for a good night's sleep. And thank you for tightening the porch floor. I've been meaning to do it myself, but haven't had the time, nor energy."

Tim woke with a smile the next morning. Content and energized, he crutched down the hallway with vigor. "Morning, Mom!" Glancing at the table, he saw not just a breakfast tin, but a handsaw. "Where did this come from?" he asked, bewildered.

She replied, "I'm not sure, it wasn't here when we settled for the night, and neither was this bag of plaster of Paris," which Tim had assumed was flour. After breakfast and pleasant conversation with his mother, he asked, "May I go sit on the porch steps for a short time?"

"Yes, but pull your hat on firmly; we don't want to catch cold right before Christmas, do we?"

Excited to meet the day, he was opening the door when he saw, on the very step he intended to rest upon, a pile of boards. *My heavens, where are these to go? I'd best move them so the snowflakes don't melt and ruin their pretty color.* It took a while, but the boards were safely stacked under the porch roof's cover.

Out of breath, he was crutching through the kitchen door in search of Mom when, before he could speak, there was a voice from above. "Build an A-shaped ladder tall enough to reach me, yet narrow enough at the base to fit through our doorways. You will be one rung short, so cut the crutch up to finish."

Instantly, Tim's thinking wheels were spinning. Six days till Christmas—it seemed an impossible task, but he was motivated by the thought that a patched ceiling would be a wonderful present for Mom. She had swept the floor often as tiny particles of plaster had fallen since his earliest childhood recollection.

Working at a pace comfortable for a weak physique and in a peaceful frame of mind, after a few days he was content with his progress under Mother's watchful eyes. When Christmas Eve evening arrived, Daddy came home from work to say, "Mr. Scrooge is coming tomorrow to inspect our home and decide whether to raise our rent or not."

Tim slid slowly into submission as reality sunk in. *I'm just doing my best*, he thought silently. *Mr. Scrooge can't raise our rent if he has a heart that beats as mine does.*

Shortly thereafter, there was a knock upon the kitchen door, then a gruff voice. "I like the porch floor and the kitchen ceiling too!" Mr. Scrooge said in an unexplainable tone. "I brought a Christmas feast, if I may share it with you fine folks."

As they sat at the table, the former Mr. Scrooge said grace and gave blessings like he'd never done. "Tim, my good man, come sit upon my knee as I thank the good Lord above for all you have taught me!" The following came, "How can I repay what has been given to me?—Now I have a family. Amen."

Enough, Dear?—*The concept of "going shopping" was first developed after the Great Exhibition of 1851. Held in the Crystal Palace in Hyde Park, May to October 1851, it was intended as a celebration of the British Empire and advances in technology. It was also instrumental in development of the tourism industry.*

The Travelers

JOY L. WILBERT ERSKINE

Orville and Marie stepped down from the carriage while the driver retrieved their two small suitcases, depositing them carefully on the sidewalk. Traveling light was easy, since they didn't have much of anything to begin with. Cambridge was a new town for them and a fresh start for the second time in as many years. This time, they hoped, it would work.

Orville had heard there was seasonal employment in Cambridge that paid well enough to put a roof over their heads all year round and take care of all their other needs. He'd been told the work was sometimes difficult, but once you passed the apprenticeship period you could count on the job as long as you wanted it. The company was growing, hiring on new workers every season since it had planted roots in Cambridge. For Orville and Marie, it sounded like a dream come true.

He fully intended to get a job and a place to finally call home, so their first stop would be at the employment office. With a little luck, they'd both be bringing in a paycheck in a week or so and their new life could begin. He and Marie were both excited at the prospect.

Retrieving their belongings, they trudged across Wheeling Avenue to the Berwick Hotel, where Orville had made arrangements for a night's lodging.

"My, what a swanky hotel," gasped Marie as she stared up at the grand building. "You'd think this was New York City!"

Orville smiled and held the door for his wife. "I thought you might like a little pampering, my dear. We might as well start our new life off on the right foot."

"Well, perhaps one night won't hurt..." she smiled gratefully up at him. "But tomorrow, we'll need to be a bit more practical."

The very next morning, before the winter sun slid into view on the horizon, the pair were dressed in their best and on their way to the employment office, excited to see what openings were available. There was already a line at the door but, undeterred, they took their place at the end and waited.

It was nearly 10 o'clock before their names were called. "Orville and Marie Reisender!" They rose from their chairs in unison. Clasping their luggage in nervous hands, they followed a pleasant-looking middle-aged woman into an interview room.

Appraising them carefully, she smiled. "Please, stand right over there, just so." They did as requested, a little confused but obedient.

"Look at me! Set your valises down a moment." They did. "Yes! You're perfect. You're required. Report to Dickens Universal at once—we have transport waiting just outside that door," she said, pointing.

A flush of relief came over Orville's face; he pumped the interviewer's hand gratefully. Marie just stood by wearing a wide smile, nodding vigorously.

"We made it!" Marie's voice burst with joy the moment the door closed behind them. "We got the job!"

"We did, my love!" Orville shouted as he lifted her from her feet and twirled her around him. "We finally have a place to call home!"

And so it was that Orville and Marie found a new life in Cambridge, Ohio, working at Dickens Universal. The work was hard, t'was true, for two months out of the year, but all they had to do was stand very, very still, almost holding their breath, in their assigned places along Wheeling Avenue. For the other ten months, they were pampered, comfortable, and very, very happy.

"Heaven knows we need never be ashamed of our tears, for they are rain upon the blinding dust of earth, overlying our hard hearts. I was better after I had cried, than before—more sorry, more aware of my own ingratitude, more gentle."

~ Charles Dickens, *Great Expectations.*

The Beggars—*Beggars were a common sight in Victorian England. Systems of relief for the poor were rudimentary and consisted of the grim prospect of the workhouse or poorhouse. Oftentimes, survival in the street was preferential over the living conditions in those places.*

Sir James of Westershire

JAMES ASP

A scene recaptured – A child with a shoeshine box,
Victorian London – a devilish time of determination, arrogance, and
poverty.

Few would cast notice of the pricy linens which adorned the young lad, as most would company him less than an indignant glance. But these tattered stitches belied a child much more than his menial presence, and openly whispered, at the least, a consciousness of former privilege. And anyone who might care as to these stained adornments would likely disregard him but a patron of wealthy charity.

His given name now lost to history, we'll call him as he called himself…Sir James—a noble title which he christened himself in selfless bereavement.

Though now of only eleven years, Sir James was a toddler when he emigrated from the Promised Land, in the capital city of Virginia. He was the only live birth to his angelic mother, Autumn Day, she an American-born slave who embodied femininity, beauty, and an undying resolve to instill in her young son a passion for life and an appetite for freedom.

Though stolen by love from the chains of bondage herself, Autumn Day was endowed with the ability to enslave admiring attention from across the most vehement of racial boundaries.

Sir James' father, Rudd, from Westershire, a small coal village southeast of Stonehenge—husband to his stolen love from beyond the sea—was a man of self-reliance, who until recent knew nothing of poverty nor, until his end, the wages of death—spending the last of his heart and silver, faithful to his afflicted bride.

And thus, a debtor's prison and a second mound on Potter's Hill were soon his earthly fate—eternally beside his darling Autumn Day.

Devoted to his mother's dreams and his father's determined legacy, the young lad took on the role of Knight to his late Queen Mother and to the man who would always be his King.

Now a child of naught, Sir James would at last fit himself in the best of the garments he could carry. He clutched his Bible and seized the wooden box by which he once shined his father's shoes.

Sir James felt no need to swallow pride; this wooden box was his Royal inheritance—a princely bestowment—and tools by which he could rebuild his castle.

It was rare in this kingdom, the abstinent clatter of a discarded coin, but an obscure quote his mother once described to him at a bedtime reading cleaved to his thoughts: "In all labor there is profit."

So it was with faithful service the former knave did seek out to bring honor upon the souls of his departed parents. As a lamb to the slaughter, he fearfully pressed nearer the busy streets of London, where the spit-soaked cobblestones glittered and litter blew to collect in every fissured eddy.

Not many rains would pass that did this lad sleep dry. For the poor in the streets were plenty. And a vagrant's shelter was seldom vacant. It seemed that Hell visited all of Europe in the last decade or so and thus spilled each of its destitute onto the isle of Britain.

At this, the boy looked in amazement at a simple potato on a cart—raw and solid—and for it he spent this day's earnings. *To imagine, that such a thing be the reason for so much suffering,* he thought to himself as he skinned it with his teeth.

Yet Sir James grinned as he thinned and treated every rancid morsel, and customer, with grace, knowing …believing…that one day he would be delivered.

Despite the florescence of his work and his concentration toward kind entreatment, the young boy became a great lark, insomuch that many began to stop and mock the self-proclaimed Knight—women even casting kerchiefs in open degradation of him. Still, Sir James was undeterred, accepting the feigned affection with the grace of a true nobleman.

One day, perhaps by providence, a patron did find a rusted helmet of iron and gently placed it cockeyed on the lad's small head—in probability an attempt to further incite public laughter.

However, delighted with the unseemly gift, the boy rubbed out all of the rust the very first evening under a full moon's light—lubricating the hinges with the oils of his trade.

Early the next day, Sir James proudly arrived with the shoeshine box at his normal location, awkwardly wearing his new shining armor. It glimmered in the amber morning sun like gold and outshone every glass window in town. Even drunken sailors, shaken awake, guarded their eyes against the omnipresent glow.

If ever a grown man be imputed with such humiliation, he might lose his dignity, but not Sir James. He sat and polished his gift at every breaking opportunity.

Soon, he was the laugh around town—"That negro boy...the Knight," they'd mock. "Sir?" The consistent satire became disheartening to the kindly Victorian women of class and they began to protest the boorish humiliation. But by this, and through his professionalism toward it, his growing notoriety began to attract new and curious patrons.

Not long after this, Sir James began to hold his first real money—though a pittance by standard, it was stone by which he could lay a foundation.

Then one winter night, as Sir James slumbered along the dark city street, his precious helmet of armor was taken by a thief. It was a horrible event, as those who watched him search in every corner, in every drain, and on every rooftop...all in vain.

Word spread fast of this intolerable deed, even made it all the way to the Queen. Mourning herself the loss of her love, she gathered her subjects, her court, and her jests, and set them on horseback to make an arrest.

The helmet of armor was soon her hands. And it was heard that a rich man did steal the thing, realizing it once belonged to a King.

Again Victoria summoned her men, and them to the boy she did immediately send. The royal guard did surround the lad, who continued to look for the armor he had. The street was now filled with red and with gold. A festival of pomp and circumstance was a sight to behold. All was quiet as the crowds did part. It was horses and saddles and flags and carts.

"James of Westershire," the Queen did announce. "Show yourself worthy now before my court."

The boy stood afraid, though as tall as he could, and approached the Queen as low as a fool.

"Are you thee who hast lost thy hat?" Victoria asked.

He knelt to reply, "Your majesty, forgive me any misdeeds. I am a selfless lad who knows no greed." The boy was sore afraid. He could not further speak, for he was very aware he'd called himself great.

The Queen approached and drew a sword. His neck did he put forth to accept its cold. He thought of his parents and how they'd be scorned; how he'd done all he could but a failure he was born.

"Are you James, son of Rudd?" she asked, "…Son of Autumn Day?"

"Yes, Your Majesty. I am he," he reluctantly replied.

"Then I now wish to thank you for your faithful service, and for the honor you have brought to your parents, your country, and your Queen," she said. And as she tapped once each shoulder, Queen Victoria announced, "I now dub you 'Sir James of Westershire, Knight of the Royal Court.'"

The queen then unwrapped his stolen helmet of armor and laid it in his arms. Sir James received half of the rich thief's property in reparation for the harm. His parents were reburied together on his new land, with their names carved in stone for all eternity:

DAY

Autumn | Rudd
1819-1857 | 1817-1860
Your loving son, James
A pauper to a Prince, I think to strike—
But poetically more…a Day to a Knight.

The Caroling Family—*The first commercial Christmas card was designed by J.C. Horsley for Henry Cole, founder of the Victoria and Albert Museum, in 1843. It was the size of an ordinary postcard.*

THE GALLAGHER FAMILY SINGERS

DONNA J. LAKE SHAFER

"**O**kay, everyone. Line up. It will soon be inspection time and we need to look our best. I thought I saw a petticoat peeking out from the hem of Lizzie's skirt this morning."

Sarah Gallagher assured her husband that the offending undergarment had been secured and their daughter was presentable. The girl had been blessed with a beautiful soprano voice and was always well behaved. It was young Mathew who occupied Sarah's mind now. He possessed a great voice, so sweet and clear, but now something was happening and she was worried. Recently, she had noticed a slight cracking when he spoke. And there was a different look about the boy these days. She couldn't quite put her finger on it, but it nagged at her. Sarah never mentioned it to her husband, but she had some serious concerns.

Her thoughts were interrupted by her quarreling children. It seems there was some misunderstanding concerning their scarves, something she must get straightened out before the spat escalated.

Charles Gallagher was very particular about how his family members presented themselves and would not abide slovenly looks or attitudes. The Dickens folks would be coming by for a final look-see in a few days. Most repairs and costume changes had taken place during the previous months but Charles always had to be satisfied himself before they were transported to their designated spots for the holiday season.

The Gallagher Family Singers were proud to be part of the Dickens Village family. They looked forward each year to entertaining the enthusiastic crowds who celebrated the joyous season of peace and goodwill by visiting the Cambridge, Ohio, Dickens Victorian Christmas Village.

Charles Gallagher surveyed his surroundings. The volunteers had been coming and going for months. It was obvious there were to be some new groups, as was usual each year. "They're certainly a talented and dedicated bunch of folks," he mused. "They're in and out of here all year long, making new costumes and repairing weather-damaged older ones, as well as making any other adjustments. The artists spend long hours creating just the right look for each of us. Amazing."

Turning once again to inspect each of his family members, he commented on Sarah's new ensemble. She looked lovely and the fur muff she held was just the right touch. Bending slightly to inspect Lizzie's face, he commented that her cheeks looked a little too "grown up" for such a young girl.

"Bosh," retorted Sarah. "Don't you think young tender skin would look flushed when standing in the cold for ages?" Conceding that his wife was probably right, he turned his attention to his young son.

"Mathew, it appears that your trousers have shrunk a bit. I hope someone notices before we leave here. And what's wrong with the sleeves on your coat? Oh dear, this will never do. Why, you look a ragamuffin!"

Mathew sulkily hung his head, remaining silent. He couldn't understand why his father went on so. *Why do these things matter so much anyway*, he wondered.

"Never mind, Charles," offered Sarah. "I'm sure someone has taken notice and these things will be corrected in due time. They always are, you know. Now just quit fussing."

Her concern was about Mathew himself rather than his attire. Some of the changes in the boy were subtle, some not. It was the voice that really bothered her. Did he have a throat problem of some sort? He hadn't complained of pain, yet she was very worried. She always made sure he kept his scarf securely around his neck. Some of the boys, she had observed, left them flapping about with a "devil-may-care" attitude, their coattails flying and hats placed jauntily on the backs of their heads. But not Mathew. He had always been very neat and tidy. Coat buttoned, scarf secure, hat placed firmly and squarely where it belonged. But now?

Sarah was sorely troubled but, not wanting to upset Charles in any way, she couldn't bring herself to bother him. His sole focus was on the coming season and the role of the Gallagher Family Singers. After all, thousands were depending upon them. The Dickens Village volunteers had given their all, as usual, and his family would do no less.

A few short days later, the big day arrived. Trucks had been rolling in to Dickens Universal all morning. There was an air of excitement as hordes of volunteers went about the business of transporting the many sets and characters to each designated destination. The Gallagher family anxiously awaited their turn. It would be so wonderful to see the amazed looks on the faces of the Dickens visitors.

Cars and busloads of folks would soon be pouring into the city and surrounding areas to see the latest wonders created by the many people who made it all possible. The Guernsey County Court House would be dressed in lighted splendor, with the carols of the season filling the air. Oh yes, it was an exciting, but stress-filled, time for all the participants. But everyone enjoyed what they were doing and took pride in the results of their labors.

Working throughout the day, the displays were in place by nightfall. They were placed all along Wheeling Avenue on the sidewalks, as well as in many store windows. A few greeted folks in other areas, including Southeastern Ohio Regional Medical Center, where the Parade of Trees would soon delight visitors. Cambridge would bustle with activity as folks enjoyed the various holiday sights, scents, and sounds.

Charles Gallagher stood proudly with his family. Glancing into each face—his lovely wife, their beautiful daughter, and handsome son—he concluded they were quite presentable. He knew they'd be in fine voice. They always were. But there was something different about his children this year. On closer inspection, he noticed that they seemed to have grown a bit taller, maybe more than a little, especially Mathew. In fact, he seemed to have lost his slightly chubby face. It looked slimmer, older.

The next evening, the people began to arrive on the streets. They wandered up and down the avenue, admiring the scenes as they enjoyed the music, the various decorations, the many activities, and, of course, the food. Everyone had the Christmas spirit and none more than the Gallagher Family Singers. During the ensuing days and weeks, they became great favorites among the crowd.

That first evening, they began their presentation with a rousing rendition of *Oh, Come All Ye Faithful*, always a favorite. Imagine their surprise and delight when young Mathew's voice rang out in a rich, strong baritone, one they had never heard. Always before, he had been the tenor of the group, but now…

With smiles and knowing glances at each other, Charles and Sarah now understood what was different about their son. He was growing up. Their little boy was becoming a man, a man whose beautiful voice would thrill the Dickens Victorian Village visitors for many years to come.

"Suffering has been stronger than all other teaching, and has taught me to understand what your heart used to be. I have been bent and broken, but –I hope—into a better shape."

~ Charles Dickens, *Great Expectations*.

The Lamplighter—*This lamplighter and his assistant perform their nightly duty. Both oil and gas burning models were used in London. In 1834, London had over six hundred miles of gas lines laid, in order to feed the street lamps. However, due to public mistrust and the high cost, these lines weren't widely used until the mid-Victorian period.*

A Tale of Two Times
The Day I Met Charles Dickens

SAMUEL D. BESKET

It was a cold Saturday in November. This was no ordinary Saturday. This was the Saturday of "The Game," the annual football game between Ohio State and Michigan.

Dan was up early, walking the dog and putting out garbage. Then he was off to Riesbeck's for game day snacks. Emerging from the store 20 minutes later, he was armed with a six-pack of Bud Light, a bucket of hot wings, and a ready-to-bake pizza.

Depositing his goodies on the kitchen counter, Dan rushed upstairs to put on his lucky jeans, his OSU sweatshirt, and his new pair of Nike TW-14 sneakers. As he settled down for the pre-game show, his wife, Beth, rushed in, clutching her cell phone and a handful of credit cards.

"I'm going shopping with Carrie. Don't forget to get the Christmas tree down from the garage attic…you promised."

"Right after the game, babe. I promise, right after the game."

As Beth rushed out the door, Dan groaned. He had been putting off getting the tree down for days. He hated that aluminum relic from the 50's. The color wheel no longer worked and half the tinsel had fallen off the metal branches, but the tree belonged to her late grandfather. He knew Beth would never part with it as long as a single branch remained intact.

As Ohio State kicked the winning field goal, Dan raced out the kitchen door into the garage, only to be greeted by a blast of cold air and leaves. *Not again,* he thought. In her haste to get to the mall, Beth forgot to close the garage door. Sweeping leaves aside, Dan closed the door and positioned his rickety old ladder between the overhead garage door tracks. Carefully climbing the steps, he opened the access door to the garage attic. Starting to squeeze through, he heard the garage door start to open.

"Oh no!" he screamed as the door started to retract. Dan frantically grabbed for an overhead rafter to pull himself into the attic. Before he could get a firm grip, the door knocked the ladder out from under him. Suddenly the garage floor came rushing up to meet him. It seemed like an eternity before his body came crashing down on the floor. After a brief second of intense pain when every joint in his body screamed, everything turned grey and his world went dark. No more pain, just nothing.

Beth sat in her car, horrified, as she watched Dan plunge to the concrete floor.

*****

Little by little, Dan regained consciousness. Small blurry orange circles flickered around the dark room. These materialized into antique candle fixtures mounted on the wall. He also realized he was naked, lying under a cover of rough woven material. As he regained his senses, a lady dressed in black with a huge white butterfly-style hat entered the room. Seeing he was awake, she walked over and sat down beside his bed.

"Be thou awake?" she asked in a strange dialect.

"Where am I?" Dan groggily replied.

"Sisters of Mercy Hospital."

"Where?"

"Thou art in Sisters of Mercy Hospital in London. Thou wert injured; now rest. The doctor will be in momentarily."

"What day is it?" Dan asked.

"Why, 'tis the twenty-second of November in the year of our Lord, 1846."

The date hit him like a Mack truck. Rising up on one elbow, the pain in his neck and shoulders forced him to lie back down. *How can this be?* he thought. *I must be dead, or hallucinating.*

"Be thou still," the lady said as she tucked in the heavy blanket. "The chemist will bring a potion for thy pain."

Dan drifted into semi-unconsciousness. In the background, as if in a fog, he could hear men talking.

"Another strange one," one voice whispered.

"I say another heretic," another voice chimed in.

"Why say thee heretic?"

"Simply by addressing his attire. The tailor's mark on his clothes reads *Made in China.* Garments of this exotic nature are not made in that heathen country. Look, no nails in his shoes; they are of one piece. I have never seen such material. 'Tis as if they were molded on his feet. The closure on his trousers, pull it up and it closes, pull it down and it opens. Definitely a heretic."

A man who appeared to be in authority suddenly drew close to Dan's face. His ruffled hair was accented by the foul smell of whiskey and tobacco on his breath.

"I say put him in with the other strange one. When he recovers, he can help with the lighting."

As they left the room, Dan heard one say, "We be prudent; they bear watching. I believe they are from another world."

During the next few weeks, Dan gradually grew stronger and accepted the fact that either he was dead or the fall had distorted his mind. He was given a smock, a pair of crude sandals, and a cape to wear. His meals consisted of a grain cooked into gruel, a piece of dark bread, and a cup of broth.

One day as Dan exercised in his room, the man with the foul breath appeared and motioned for Dan to follow. They walked down a long, dark corridor until the man stopped, opening a door. Motioning Dan inside, he said, "He calleth himself Tommy; work with him as a luminary." With that, he left.

After a minute of staring at each other, the man walked to Dan. Whispering, "Be careful; they may be listening," he pointed to a far corner. Sitting on a straw mattress, they began to talk.

"I'm Tommy Shelby. What's your name?"

"Dan George." Dan was excited to hear someone speak a language he could understand. "Where are we?" he asked. "Are we dead? Is this hell or purgatory?"

"We're in London, in the constable's stable, or jail in our world."

"Jail!" Dan shouted, quickly putting his hand over his mouth.

After talking non-stop for a few hours, the two discovered the only thing they had in common was serving in the Air Force. Dan finally broached the subject of how they arrived at this location.

"I believe we were translated," Tommy stated.

"Translated?"

"Yes, like when you die, your soul goes to heaven or hell. I believe our whole bodies were translated to…wherever we are."

"How did you get here?"

"A tornado. I lived in a small town in Broken Bow, Oklahoma. I was awakened by a fierce wind and my wife screaming, "Tornado!" I ran for the basement. The last thing I remember the roof blew off and I was sucked up in the air. I woke up here. How did you get here?"

Dan explained how he fell getting the Christmas tree down from the attic. "How do we get back? Can we escape?" he asked.

"I tried it once; there is no place to go. I think it's best if we play dumb, lest we be thrown into an insane asylum. Now put on your cape; you can help me light the street lamps."

As they walked out of the stable, Tommy cautioned Dan about the new world he was about to encounter.

"London in December is a cold, dark, damp place. You'll see people in all forms of dress and stature—aristocrats in their tall hats and long waistcoats accompanying women in hoopskirts, capes, and birdcage hats; the common folks, shuffling along dressed in smocks, barely uttering a word. Just follow my lead."

Leaving the building, Dan was shocked at 19th Century London. The dreary atmosphere was capped by the pungent odor of horse manure and unwashed bodies. As they rounded a corner, a large white ornate carriage accompanied by a troupe of soldiers galloped by. Tom stopped and bowed from the waist. "Bow, bow," he whispered as the carriage sped by. "It's Queen Victoria. It's best we bow, better than risk a lash across the face."

As they walked along the street, lighting lamp after lamp, Tom continued to educate Dan on how to survive in this ancient atmosphere. Their task completed, they made their way back toward the constable's stable. As they approached a large hall, sounds of laughter filled the damp night air.

"What goes on?" Dan inquired.

"Charles Dickens is giving a recital."

"Charles Dickens!"

"Yes, the one you hated to read in high school literature."

As they drew nearer, Dan couldn't control his emotions. He ran up the steps and peeked through a crack in the door. At center stage stood Charles Dickens. He was a short man by modern standards, balding, with a thin scraggly beard, but his voice bellowed throughout the building. As Dan inched the door open to get a better look, a large hand grabbed him by the shoulder and spun him around. Facing him was a large man dressed in black with a star over his left breast pocket.

"Let's be off, you rummy old cove," the constable shouted as he shoved Dan down the steps. As Dan picked himself up, Tommy was quickly by his side.

"You crazy man, you're lucky you didn't get your skull cracked…now let's go."

Safely back, Tommy scolded Dan for his rash act.

"I couldn't help it, Tommy. I've read several of Charles Dickens novels. Cambridge, the town I live in some hundred-and-sixty years from now, goes all-out for Dickens at Christmas. I want to see more…I have to see more."

"Well, there is a way, but you have to be more careful."

"What do you mean by 'a way'?"

"Through the basement. I was there once, emptying the privy barrels. But be careful."

The next morning as they extinguished the streetlights, Tommy pointed to a small door leading to the hall's basement.

"It stinks down there, but if you want to see Dickens, it's the safest vantage point."

Everything stinks here, Dan thought.

Daylight revealed a London even more depressing than it was at night. People used the street as a sewer to dispose of everything from dishwater to garbage. Smoke and fog hung over the city, virtually blocking out the sun.

The next night, their lighting task completed, Dan crept down the building's narrow basement steps and gently pushed the door open. Slowly walking across the room, he noticed a small beam of light showing through a loose overhead board. Climbing onto a barrel, he gently pulled back the loose board. There, standing just a few yards above him, was Charles Dickens, giving a synopsis of David Copperfield. Dan was mesmerized. He could hear Dickens booming voice echo throughout the hall.

When the performance was completed, Dan carefully replaced the board and slithered out the basement and back to the constable's stable. He had a hard time controlling his emotions as he described the performance to Tommy.

During the next few weeks, Dan heard renditions of *Oliver Twist*, *A Tale of Two Cities*, and numerous critiques of local characters and society. Then came the night of Dickens' final performance, a rendering of *A Christmas Story*. Dan stacked another barrel on his perilous perch for a better view. When Dickens entered the stage, he was greeted by thunderous applause and shouts of "Hear, hear."

Walking to center stage, Dickens raised his hands for quiet. As he did, a small button popped off his coat and rolled a few inches from Dan's view. Shifting his weight to one side, Dan reached for the button. It was then that his makeshift perch collapsed and hurled him to the floor. Once again Dan's world went from pain to a deadly silence, then darkness.

*****

Awakening, Dan was surrounded by machines, flashing green lights, and beeping sounds. As his mind cleared, he ran his hand over his face, only to discover he had a beard. Little by little, he regained his senses and it all became clear. He remembered falling while getting the Christmas tree from the attic. His thoughts were interrupted by a young nurse entering the room.

"Where am I?" Dan blurted out.

Startled, the nurse turned and smiled. "Well, welcome back, Mr. George. You're in Southeastern Med. You had a long nap. I'll call the doctor and tell your wife."

After a few minutes of poking and prodding, the doctor nodded his head. "You'll be fine. I'll have the nurses unhook you from all these machines and then we'll get you up in a chair. Remember, you've been in a coma for four weeks. You'll be weak, but soon you should be as good as new."

Finally, everyone left and Beth was quickly by his side. "I'm so sorry, honey," she said with teary eyes. "I didn't know you were on the ladder when I put the door up."

"Don't blame yourself. It was my fault. I should have turned the electric off to the door. Did the doctor say four weeks? Well, that explains the beard. I had the strangest dream, honey. I dreamed I was in London in 1846. It was so lifelike. I met a fellow from Oklahoma. I saw Charles Dickens. I...I...I'm confused; it was so real."

Sitting on the bed, Beth cupped Dan's face in her hands.

"You were delusional. It's the result of the concussion. You were mumbling something about Queen Victoria, Charles Dickens, and someone named Tommy the whole time you were in the coma. The doctor said it's common with head injuries."

Standing up, Beth ran her hands through her hair. "I'm going home for a shower. Can I bring you something?"

"Yes, a Dickens novel."

"How about David Copperfield?"

Dan nodded his head in agreement. As Beth walked out of the room, Dan spied a phone on a small table. After a few minutes, propped up on one elbow, he dialed directory assistance.

"What city, please?"

"Broken Bow, Oklahoma."

"What residence?"

"Thomas Shelby."

"For an additional fifty cents, I can connect you, sir."

"That would be great."

As the phone rang, Dan concocted a story to conceal his true intentions.

"Shelby residence, this is Brittany."

"Hi Brittany, you don't know me. My name is Dan George. I was stationed with a Tom Shelby when I was in the Air Force. I was wondering if this is the same Tom Shelby residence."

"It's strange you called; I was just going through some of Tom's things. Yes, he was in the Air Force."

"Going through Tom's things?" Steve inquired.

"Yes, Tom was killed in a tornado three years ago. His body was never found."

Stunned by the news, Dan fell back into the bed and stared at the ceiling.

As Beth walked into the room, she was shocked by Dan's appearance. "You okay? You look like you saw a ghost."

"We need to talk."

"Me first," Beth uttered. "Just a minute. Ah…here it is."

As Dan watched, Beth pulled a small antique button from her purse and laid it on the bed. "You were clutching this in your hand when the EMT's brought you in. Do you know where it came from? It looks really old."

Dan quickly sat up and stared at the button. As he slowly sank back into the bed, he curled up in a ball and mumbled, "Oh, my God! It's true. It's true."

Queen Victoria—*Alexandria Victoria was born 24 May 1819 at Kensington Palace to Edward, Duke of Kent, and Victoria of Saxe-Coburg. She kept a diary for most of her adult life, chronicling both her personal and professional achievements.*

BEING QUEEN FOR A DAY

HARRIETTE McBRIDE ORR

Dickens Victorian Village was again set up on the streets of downtown Cambridge, ushering in the holiday season. Wheeling Avenue resembled Merry Olde England, with all of the costumed mannequins gracing the street.

Thirteen-year-old Jennie was headed to the courthouse square to wait for her ride home from the Art Guild. Since the start of the school year, she had been taking instruction in watercolor on Monday evenings. Tonight, her instructor, Ms. Sue, had told the class that the Art Guild was holding a contest to see who could create the best painting of a Dickens scene or mannequin.

The winners of the contest would ride in the Queen's Parade as part of Queen Victoria's court. This holiday season, the "Queen" would be flying in from Galveston, Texas, to be part of the Dickens Victorian Village activities.

Purchasing hot chocolate from a street vendor, Jennie found an empty bench near East 8th Street where she could watch for her mother while enjoying the free Christmas light show, set up and maintained compliments of AVC Communications.

Glancing up at the U.S. Bank building, she watched the huge wreaths as the lights danced and changed color to the beat of the Christmas music. Her eyes wandered to the corner window that overlooked Wheeling Avenue.

Spotlighted there was a mannequin portraying Victoria, Queen of England, during Charles Dickens' lifetime.

The Queen was dressed in an elegant black satin gown. The jeweled gold crown on her head completed the look of royalty. One had no doubt that she was indeed *The Queen*. From her lofty perch, she seemed to be surveying her kingdom.

Just then, Jennie's mother pulled up to the curb and Jenny hurried to get into the car.

"Mother, I was thinking about the Queen up there in the bank window. She's so removed from everything, all alone. Do you know anything about her? Did she have a family? How long was she Queen of England?"

"Jennie, if you want to know all of these things, you need to look her up on the internet. I'm sure you'll find all the information you're asking about."

When they got home, Jennie put away her art materials and finished up her homework. She then Googled "Queen Victoria."

Several sites popped up. Choosing one, she proceeded to read about the Queen. As she read, she took notes:

"Born in 1819, Victoria, the only daughter of King George III's fourth son, was only 18 when she became Queen. Her reign lasted for 63 years, the longest of any British monarch. This period in time became known as the Victorian Age, with high moral values and the rise of the middle class.

"As a child, Victoria lived a very secluded life in Kensington Palace. Her father had passed away when she was quite small. Her mother came under the influence of her lover, Lord Conroy. He insisted that little Victoria be trained in a very restrictive lifestyle. She had no one but her mother to depend on. She was never allowed to be

with other children or to learn of the great poverty most of England suffered. Lord Conroy's controlling influence became known as the Kensington System.

"When she became Queen, Victoria was still living with her mother, as was the custom of the day. Lord Melbourne, the prime minister, was another guiding force behind Victoria, teaching her the ins and outs of government. He wanted Victoria away from the influence of her mother and Lord Conroy.

"Melbourne introduced the Queen to several available suitors. The one that became her husband was her cousin, Prince Albert of Saxe-Coburg Gotha. She fell head over heels in love with Albert and she proposed to him. They were soon married and her mother and Sir Conroy were sent out of the palace by now-Queen Victoria.

"Albert was the very first person to truly show Victoria love and affection and she dearly loved him in return. They had nine children and were married only 21 years when Albert became ill with typhoid fever and passed away. His death sent Victoria into deep mourning. She wore black for the rest of her life. For years, she neglected her duties and was never seen in public. This caused her subjects to turn against her.

"During her Golden and Diamond Jubilee years, Queen Victoria forced herself to again go out among her subjects, regaining their love and admiration.

"At her death in 1901, she was hailed as an 'exemplary monarch.'"

"Jennie, you need to turn in," Mother called up the steps. "It's getting late. Turn off that computer and get to bed, young lady. Morning will come too soon. I'll be right up to tuck you in."

When mother came in the bedroom to kiss her goodnight, Jennie told her what she had learned about Queen Victoria. "I'm going to paint the Queen as my project for the art contest."

As she drifted off to sleep, Jennie couldn't help but think of Queen Victoria. She could hear music. Soon there were ladies in beautiful ball gowns and men in long frock coats waltzing round and round. Then the trumpets sounded and in came Queen Victoria and Prince Albert. The orchestra struck up the British national anthem, "God Save the Queen," as people bowed and curtsied. When the anthem ended, the couple took their chairs in the front of the room and people resumed their chatting.

As the orchestra started playing "The Blue Danube," Prince Albert took Queen Victoria's hand, bowed, and escorted her to the dance floor, where they danced, to the enjoyment of everyone. They were still dancing as Jennie awoke to the sound of her alarm clock.

At breakfast she told her mother of her dream. "My painting of Queen Victoria will be the best that I can do. I'm so excited I can hardly wait to get started."

"Jennie, I have a friend that works at U.S. bank. I'm sure she can get an okay for us to take pictures of the Queen. You need to get views of the front, each side, and even the back so that you know what she looks like from all sides."

"Oh, Mother, that'll be wonderful. It's really hard to see all of her from the street."

Jennie and her mother went to the bank the next day after school. They were met by her mother's friend, who took them upstairs, where they took pictures of Queen Victoria. They picked the four best ones and had them made into poster size.

Jennie hung them in her room and set up her easel and paints to tackle the painting. She worked every evening after her homework and all of her spare time over the weekend. On Sunday evening, she invited her mother in to take a look.

"Oh Jennie, it's gorgeous. You did such a good job. I love it!"

"Do you think it's good enough to be a winner?" Jennie asked.

"Yes! Yes, I do. We'll take it down to the Art Guild when I get off work tomorrow evening."

On Monday evening, Jennie carefully placed her painting in the back of their SUV and they were off to the Art Guild. Mother helped her fill out the entry forms and Ms. Sue placed her painting on an easel near the front window.

"Yours is the first one turned in, Jennie. You did a great job. Your work is very good. I'm so very proud of you. The judging will take place on Thursday. I will call you when it is over. Good luck."

Two weeks later, when the winners of the art contest were announced, Jennie won first prize in her age group.

Today was the Queen's parade. Jennie and her mother were invited to brunch at the Gross Mansion, where Jennie and the other winners would be presented to the Queen.

Aunt Connie and Jennie's mother had been working all week on a dress for the occasion. Their creation was an off-the-shoulder, robin's egg blue satin, with tiers of ruffles making up the very full skirt. The bodice was trimmed in yards of lace, adorned with tiny blue and pearl beads. Underneath the skirt was a hooped petticoat and white pantaloons trimmed in eyelet lace. On her feet Jennie was wearing blue satin slippers. Looking at herself in the mirror, she couldn't believe her eyes. She practiced doing her curtsey.

Mother added a fur jacket they had borrowed from the Imagination Station in "The Olde Curiosity Shoppe" and a matching fur muff.

"Wait, I think I hear the mail. I'll be right back." When she came back into the room, Mother said, "It finally came. I have a surprise for you. Here, open this."

Jennie took the box her mother handed her and read, *Tina's Tiaras*. Excitedly, she tore open the package. Inside, she found a beautiful tiara in shades of blue and pearl beads to match her dress. "Oh, thank you, thank you, Mother. It's truly beautiful. It makes me feel like a queen."

"Well, I must say it completes your outfit. Now, let's go meet the Queen."

Off they went to brunch, where the contest winners were honored by being presented to the Queen. One at a time, they curtsied or bowed and then stood by the easel displaying their winning art work.

At one-thirty, horses and open carriages arrived at the mansion. The Queen was seated in the front limousine carriage with her footmen. The contest winners rode in two carriages following along behind the Queen. They headed for Clark Street, where the parade started at the top of Wheeling Avenue. The Queen and her court were the last ones to enter the parade.

Jennie was so excited and had such fun waving to friends along the way. She thought to herself, *This has to be the most wonderful time of my life. I can hardly believe that this is happening.*

When the carriages arrived at the street fair on Seventh Street, Queen Victoria was seated on a platform with her footmen standing guard. The contest winners were seated around her as part of her formal court. Here they were entertained by jugglers, musicians, and acrobats. When the festivities of the day were over, the Queen left the street fair in her open carriage, waving to all as she passed by.

Jennie looked for her mother and Aunt Connie. When she found them, she hugged them both and thanked them for all their hard work in making this day so special for her.

"Today will be something I'll remember always. I have this painting of Queen Victoria to remind me every time I see it that it was fun being Queen for a day. But being Queen is not for me. I just love being Jennie, every day."

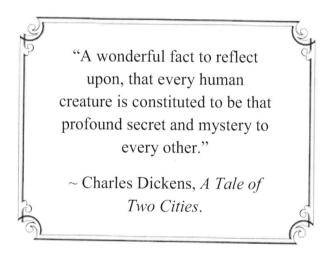

"A wonderful fact to reflect upon, that every human creature is constituted to be that profound secret and mystery to every other."

~ Charles Dickens, *A Tale of Two Cities*.

Lamplighter at Work—*The lamplighter, an employee of the town, usually used a wick on a long pole to ignite the gas flame. Lamplighters also served in the dual role of night watchman in many communities.*

A Gift to Remember

BEVERLY J. JUSTICE

Albert Beckman observed the winter landscape as a passenger, not a doting father. Debra always had been sensitive to criticism and he did not want to make her nervous. *She drives remarkably well,* he thought, *considering she earned her learner's permit only weeks ago.*

He turned an admiring grin toward his daughter. Sheer terror gripped him like a crushing vice. This woman had crow's feet, wrinkles, and graying hair. Where was Debra? Albert opened his mouth to shout at the stranger but stopped when he noticed his hand. It was hideous, with knotted knuckles and brown spots the size of quarters. He wiggled his fingers. Yes, it was his hand, all right. How could that be?

Albert slinked down into the seat as reality and memory grasped him. He was not a vigorous man of forty-four; he was eighty. *Eighty!* And Debra was no bouncy sixteen-year-old, but a fifty-two-year-old divorcee with a son in college. They were not going home to the modest brick house with a porch swing. There would be no smiling wife wiping her hands on her apron to greet him with a hug and a kiss. His home was now a room in a nursing home ("health care center" was the euphemism nowadays), with a roommate named Bob who kept jelly beans under his pillow and wore suspenders with his pajamas.

"Everything okay, Dad?" Debra asked, sensing his uneasiness.

"Fine," he answered, touching her hand. "I was just thinking how fast time flies." Albert took a deep breath and glanced at his wristwatch. *Four o'clock and nearly dark already.* "Now, where are we going again?"

"Dad, I told you before," Debra scolded. "We're going to my home in Cambridge. I've lived there for years—you know that!"

"Sorry," Albert muttered. So what if he couldn't remember the town in which she lived? She had no right to talk to him as if he were a child. Staff at the nursing home did that, too. "Dinnertime, Honey!" they'd say, or "Don't go to bed until you take your medicine." *How dare they?* Albert seethed. *I don't need kids calling me 'Honey' and telling me when to go to bed! When I was their age, I called older people 'Sir' or 'Ma'am!'*

"Dakota should be home when we arrive, Dad."

"Good," Albert answered. "He goes to Oberlin, right?"

"That's right! Good! He's a junior this year."

She shouldn't have been so surprised, Albert fumed in silence. *I'm just a little forgetful; I haven't lost my mind entirely! Speaking of minds, what in the world was she thinking when she named her only child 'Dakota?'*

Snowflakes began to wander aimlessly in the crisp air as the car slowed for the exit ramp. A few minutes later, Debra parked the car on a downtown street.

"Listen carefully, Dad," she said in her mother-mode voice. "I have to see Della at the Outer Edge Beauty Salon. I'm giving her a box for the church rummage sale. I'll only be gone for five minutes or so. I want you to promise me that you will stay in the car and not get out. I'll leave on the auxiliary power so you'll have heat. *Promise* me that you'll stay in the car."

"Oh, go run your errand," Albert answered with a wave of his hand. "I'll be fine." He watched his daughter clip-clop in her high-heeled boots up the street toward the salon.

"Five minutes, my eye!" he muttered. "Those two will be gossiping for an hour."

Albert looked at the corner that intersected Wheeling Avenue. "What in the world are those guys doing?" he wondered aloud.

Two men, decked in top hats and long coats, were standing at the base of a ladder. Another man, perched precariously upon the uppermost rung, reached toward the top of a lamp.

"That fool is going to fall! I've got to stop him."

Albert exited the car and hurried to the scene. In his excitement, he forgot to bring his cane. *I don't need that thing anyhow,* he protested. *I only use it so Debra won't nag at me.*

He was about to give the men a lecture on safety when he stopped in his tracks. Albert slowly extended a finger to one man's beard. Plaster! The men were mannequins dressed in Victorian garb, depicting the scene of lamplighters of that era.

Albert chuckled, then looked around. The entire downtown looked like a village in which Charles Dickens himself would feel at home: Victorian women in all their finery carrying wrapped packages, carolers with top hats and fur capes, a Victorian policeman keeping order. Albert noticed a shop nearby called "Ye Olde Antique Shoppe." He stepped inside.

"Good afternoon, Sir," a young woman greeted him, with a smile as bright as sunshine itself. Albert thought how glad he felt to be called "Sir" instead of "Honey."

"May I help you with something, Sir?"

"Oh, I'm just looking. I haven't been in Cambridge for a while. What's with the old-fashioned fake people?"

"This is our eighth year of the Victorian Village," the girl told him. "Most of the downtown buildings were built during the Victorian Era and are a perfect backdrop for the tableaus."

"Unique!" exclaimed Albert. "Look at this!" he said, picking up a kitchen utensil. "An old-fashioned potato masher! My mother—and my grandmother—used one just like this."

"A lot of people buy old utensils like that to hang on their kitchen walls for decoration. My name is Allie, by the way."

"Glad to meet you, Allie. I'm Albert. What have we here?"

He walked toward a shelf of old toys. A little tin fire truck and a wooden horse pull-toy occupied him for a moment. And then he saw it. His audible gasp caught Allie's attention.

"Did you find something, Albert?"

Albert clutched a rag doll in front of him. The red yarn pigtails were somewhat faded and the bloomers needed a good bleaching. But otherwise this doll was identical to Miss Annie.

It was the Christmas after Debra's sixth birthday. She, her mother, and Albert had finished opening their gifts and were about to have breakfast. Albert, standing next to the Christmas tree and holding one arm behind his back, sang, "Debra, Debra, eyes so blue; look what Santa brought for you!" He no sooner pulled the doll from behind him when Debra, squealing with joy, grabbed the doll and embraced it in a tight hug.

"I'll name her Miss Annie and I'll keep her forever!"

It was a promise Debra nearly kept. Miss Annie saw her through skinned knees, countless best friends, her first crush, and even college. But somewhere between marriage and Dakota's birth, Miss Annie became lost forever. Until now.

"I want this doll, Allie."

"Good choice, Albert. I'll wrap her in tissue paper and put her in a bag for you."

Albert opened his wallet, pulling out a bill. He saw the number "50" on it but couldn't understand for the life of him what it meant, reminding him of the time he couldn't find lettuce in the grocery even though he'd bought it dozens of times before.

Panic began to set in when Allie said, "Don't worry—I can change that for you." She took the fifty-dollar bill and returned some change. She handed the bag with the doll to Albert and said, "Sir, may you have a very Merry Christmas."

"That I will, young lady; that I will. And I wish you a Merry Christmas, too." Allie beamed a luminous smile as Albert headed for the door.

He stood on the sidewalk, wondering which way to the car. He noticed the mannequins with the stepladder and remembered that the car was down the street from them. As he turned the corner, he saw Debra pacing frantically.

"Dad!" she screamed upon seeing him. "You promised you'd stay in the car!" Her face was drenched with tears.

Albert reached into the bag and began singing, "Debra, Debra, eyes so blue; look what Santa brought for you."

She unwrapped the tissue, then put her hand to her mouth.

"Miss Annie!" she whispered. "How did you ever find another Miss Annie?"

"A father always knows what his little girl wants. Even when she isn't little anymore."

Debra and her father embraced as snowflakes danced around them. Miss Annie's button eyes twinkled in the lamplight. "Christmas miracles not only occur in Cambridge Victorian Village," Debra whispered into her father's ear. "They're expected."

ЖRDФРЖ

Christmas Harmony—*"O Come All Ye Faithful" was the most popular carol of 1843. That same year, Charles Dickens wrote and published "A Christmas Carol."*

A CHRISTMAS MOUSE HOUSE

DICK METHENEY

The sidewalk felt bitter cold outside the burning house. Red lights flashed; sirens blared. Firefighters were shouting and running in every direction, some dragging hoses from their big red truck, others attempting to smash through the front door. Another group was spraying water everywhere. Pedro Sanchez was terrified. That was his house on fire.

Well, it was not exactly his house; in addition to him and his family residing in the basement, it also housed an attorney's office and several apartments on the second and third floors. With his ever-increasing family, a suitable home was going to be very difficult to find. Pedro needed a miracle, and fast.

Fortunately, he had taken Carmela and the children out to dinner when the house caught fire. After enjoying a sumptuous meal in the alley behind Kennedy's Bakery, they were almost home when they were nearly crushed by the fire engines. He and Carmela quickly herded the children under the porch of a neighboring building and watched in horror as their home was destroyed by flames.

Hours later, with the firefighters and their trucks and hoses all gone, Pedro and Carmela sent the children to stay with a neighbor and entered the building to see if there was anything they could salvage. There was nothing left. Everything they owned was burnt, covered in soot and ash, or washed away by the fire hoses. Their little nook in the basement was inundated with two feet of debris-laden water.

As Pedro and Carmela tried to make their way to the neighbor's house, they were nearly captured by the mean old tomcat that lived two doors down the street. They had to make a mad dash for safety, with Pedro leading the race. Desperate, he scurried up the pant leg of a man standing on the corner of Ninth Street and Wheeling Avenue, with Carmela right behind him. Fortunately for everyone, it was one of the Dickens mannequins, not a real human.

Old Tom was determined to have mouse for dinner. Hissing and snarling, he attacked the mannequin, trying to tear his way through the clothing and padding. The cat was so involved in trying to catch Pedro and Carmela he failed to notice a somewhat inebriated man weaving his way down the street.

The man, Glenn Johnson, was studiously making his way down Wheeling Avenue toward his apartment when he observed the large yellow cat attacking a man standing on the street corner. Glenn instantly whipped off his John Deere baseball cap and began striking the cat to distract it from its intended victim, all the while yelling for help at the top of his lungs. Old Tom yowled his frustration and fled the scene.

Patting the victim on the shoulder to console him, Glenn noticed the rigid posture of the mannequin and muttered, "The poor fellow must have been scared stiff by that nasty old mountain lion." Having recently moved to Cambridge from Colorado to work on the oil rigs, Glenn was used to seeing mountain lions. As he staggered on down the street, he observed, "Huh! I don't know why he was so scared; it was just a little mountain lion."

Perched on a wooden two-by-four and surrounded by carpet padding, Pedro and Carmela had clung fearfully to each other throughout the episode. Anxious to get back to their children and exhausted by all the events, the two of them crept down the pants leg to peek out. They could hear Old Tom snuffling and grumbling in the alley, just waiting for them to let their guard down. The couple quietly went back up into their cozy little haven and eventually fell asleep, but not without some recurring nightmares of ferocious cats chasing them.

Pedro woke up when the sidewalk traffic increased in the morning. Normally, he and Carmela were daytime sleepers, not getting up until late afternoon. They always spent the rest of the evening and night providing for their family. However, as the noise had amplified, he decided to explore the mannequin's inner workings while the exhausted Carmela slept.

The space was really quite small, much smaller than their residence in the basement, but it had possibilities. With some minor modifications, they should be able to make do until their home was rebuilt. It was close to their former home; Pedro would be able to keep an eye on the reconstruction and prevent some other mouse family from moving into his space.

He related all this to Carmela when she awoke much refreshed in the late afternoon. His wife gave the inside of the mannequin a doubtful glance and said, "I don't know, dear. This is November and it gets quite cold in this part of the world in winter. It is not like our former home in South Texas."

Back in Texas, their attraction for each other had created an uproar between their families. His parents had thought her family was too highbrow and uppity, while her folks just knew the Sanchez's did not have the same social status as the Camarilla's. So, tired of the squabbling and fussing, the two of them had simply eloped. They had been married by a Justice of the Peace named Lawrence Mousegrave.

For their honeymoon, Pedro had located a cozy little nook in a four-inch pipe that was stacked in a pile of similar pipes in a supply terminal. Other than an occasional prowling rattlesnake, it was a nice enough place. Then, without any warning, their honeymoon suite had been loaded onto an eighteen-wheeler. Before a mouse could say, "No way, Jose," they were on their way to Cambridge, Ohio. Carmela often reminded him of his unfortunate choice of a place for their honeymoon.

It had taken some adjustments for them to get used to the climate and different customs in their new home. South Texas was hot, dry, and brown the year around, while Cambridge had more rainfall and seasons. There were more people and cats, but not so many snakes and no tarantulas.

Pedro was content in their new town, but Carmela was prone to periodic attacks of homesickness. These bouts of depression seemed to ease up when the first of their several groups of children were born.

The problem they faced now was, where were they going to live until their basement apartment was rebuilt? In all likelihood, it would take weeks, or even months, before it would be possible to move back. While Carmela worried about how her children would take to moving into a new home, Pedro simply allowed his Latino laid-back nature to come to the forefront.

He said, "Carmela, my love, we will tell the children we are going to be camping out for a while. This mannequin's hollow body is not very large, but there is quite enough room for all of us."

"But Christmas is coming and the children are going to expect presents. There is not even a chimney for Santa to come down on Christmas Eve. It is November and it's going to get cold at night. There is no way to heat this mannequin. The children will catch cold, or worse, pneumonia."

Pedro said, "The children are stronger than you think. They will be excited about a campout. We will get a tree and some decorations. It will be just like our first Christmas together."

"I certainly hope not. I nearly froze into a Popsicle, it was so cold."

"It was not that bad, darling. Yes, it sometimes did get a little nippy that first winter. We had our love to keep us warm, didn't we?"

Carmela added, a little sarcastically, "Yes, we had our love and then lots of chilly little children."

"Yes, and they are such cute children, and you have to admit they are a blessing."

Carmela warmed a little. "Yes, they are a blessing…but our neighbor is already blessed with a large family; by now she will be frazzled. I'll go pick up the children. You see if you can find some extra bedding for us."

"You watch out for Old Tom. That mangy cat is determined to have mouse for breakfast, lunch, and dinner."

Pedro found several discarded napkins in a nearby trash can and, as he reduced them to a manageable size, he made his plans to find a tree and decorations. It wouldn't be Christmas without a tree. He knew it was going to be difficult for Carmela to get along in such a small space; she had come from a very well-to-do family and never had to cope with much adversity. His family, on the other hand, had always been poor and he had learned how to survive at an early age.

The Sanchez family soon had a comfortable home established in the group of Dickens mannequins right outside their former home. Pedro and several of the older boys had made a perilous journey to locate and bring back a two-inch long piece of pine bough. It was much too big to get up the pant leg they used for an entrance, but fit quite easily under the voluminous skirts of a female mannequin. A few trips to the alley behind Kennedy's Bakery provided colored sugar sprinkles and bits of tinsel for decorations.

Even Carmela was impressed with how good the tree looked. She had been busy storing pieces of nuts and candy to be used for Christmas presents for the children.

The whole family joined in to find and store supplies for the winter. In the cold of winter Old Tom did not prowl so much, but any snow accumulation made it difficult for the mouse family to travel very far to find food. Therefore, they needed to have an adequate amount stored for the coldest months.

Christmas was maybe not as festive as in years past, but the children enjoyed the gifts and the caroling that went on throughout the holiday season.

After a gala New Year's Eve party, life became more of a struggle for the Sanchez family. Nothing had been done to start rebuilding their former home and Pedro was worried. What would they do if the building was demolished? To make matters worse, the weather turned bad and it got colder every night. Carmela and the children stayed huddled together under a heavy layer of bedding in order to keep from freezing.

Pedro struggled to keep food on the table and search for a new home. The only places available were down on the lower end of town and he knew Carmela was too proud to move into that kind of neighborhood.

One cold frosty Saturday morning, after a long night of searching the frozen streets for some sort of suitable housing for his family, a crew of humans came down the street, loading the mannequins into pickup trucks and vans. Before he had time to warn his family, their mannequin was lifted into a warm van and they were transported to a huge warehouse off Woodlawn Avenue.

Their mannequin was off-loaded and stored with what seemed like a hundred others in the south end of a large room. It was not balmy by any stretch of the imagination, but it was much warmer than the nine hundred block of Wheeling Avenue. After a little time to get settled in, the Sanchez family began enjoying the Ohio winter in the relative comfort of that old warehouse.

For the first time in their marriage, Carmela was happy with their living arrangements. "This is wonderful, Pedro," she squealed in delight. "It's almost as big as Mamacita Camarilla's home in Texas, and we don't have to worry about Old Tom here either. I'm sorry I doubted you, my love. You have provided for our family very well."

At last, the miracle he had hoped for. Pedro just smiled.

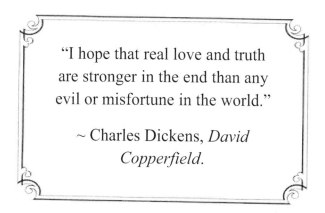

"I hope that real love and truth are stronger in the end than any evil or misfortune in the world."

~ Charles Dickens, *David Copperfield.*

Night at the Theatre—*Victorian theatres were known for their elaborate sets and lighting. The visual aspect of a play or opera was considered just as important as the script or actors. Often entire scenes were done with only expressions, no movement. These were referred to as "tableaus."*

Magical Sleigh Ride

BEVERLY WENCEK KERR

Tap, tap, tap! The sound of Joe's hammer, hitting the anvil as he shaped the horseshoes, rang out from the corner of 10th Street and Wheeling Avenue. Everyone knew Joe's Blacksmith Shoppe was the best spot in town for horseshoe repair. Joe bent over his anvil, shaping the horseshoe carefully so it would be a perfect fit for the horse of Stephen, a friend who drove a beautiful white gold-trimmed carriage through the streets of Cambridge.

The holiday season in Dickens Victorian Village made this an especially profitable time and Joe enjoyed the magic of the season. His chest nearly burst with pride as he watched the horses he had shod prancing up and down Wheeling Avenue, pulling lovely carriages filled with people in the holiday spirit.

"Hello, Joe! How go the shoes for Nellie?" Stephen perched himself on a stool near the forge, holding Nellie's reins while Joe put the finishing touches on the shoes for Stephen's horse. "Nellie really needs those shoes tonight. The streets are going to be busy with the Chocolate Walk and the Christmas show. It should be a good chance to fill my pockets with some coins."

"Don't get yourself in a stew. You need to be more easy-going, like old Nellie here." Joe straightened his back and stretched slowly before bending back down to finish the job. "Nellie's shoes will be ready to hammer on in a minute. That is one fine horse you have, and very patient."

"Ah, yes, Nellie's the best! She's gentle as a lamb with the children and ladies. When she prances down the street, sometimes it seems like her hooves barely touch the ground."

Joe put the final nail in Nellie's shoes, then watched with pride as Stephen hitched her to the carriage and headed down Wheeling Avenue.

*****

Tap, tap, tap! On a cold bench outside the theater, Katherine tapped her foot, impatiently waiting for the show to begin. A warm coat with a red knit scarf kept the winter chill from bothering her. Christmas always brought her out to watch the crowds pass on their way to shop for the holidays. But Katherine didn't need to shop, she only wanted to see the Christmas show.

While she waited, she heard the clip-clop of a horse's hooves. *Riding in a horse and carriage would be more fun than playing charades,* thought the young lady. The next time she heard it, she jumped from the bench to the side of the street.

"Any chance you could take a lady for a short ride?" Katherine smiled as she approached the carriage driver, Stephen.

"Usually people pay to ride, but I'm in the Christmas spirit tonight, so let me help you up here." Stephen placed a warm blanket over Katherine's legs before heading off on an adventure.

Katherine and the carriage just seemed to float over the town, almost like a magic carpet with sleigh bells attached. Stephen's eyes opened wide with wonder as he felt the sleigh actually lift from the ground. *Wow!* he thought. *Nothing like this ever happened before. Joe must really have a magical touch.*

Looking down, Katherine could see all the mannequins along the street. And there were the beautiful courthouse lights she'd heard so much about but never seen. Katherine's laughter warmed the air as she pleaded with the driver, "Could you circle around again so I can see the lights a little better? Slow down!"

Stephen settled the carriage softly on the roof of the bank, then watched with Katherine, enjoying the pulsating courthouse Christmas lights, synchronized to holiday music. Crowds of people gathered in front of the courthouse, with children dancing on the courthouse lawn. What a beautiful sight to behold!

Later, as they drifted over the city, Stephen swooped low over Joe's Blacksmith Shoppe. With a tilt of the sleigh, he waved to a smiling Joe, standing there looking as proud as punch.

Katherine was as excited as the kids at a chestnut roasting when the sleigh glided over Cambridge City Park. Christmas lights, decorating homes all over town, glittered like diamonds and rubies as their twinkling lights reflected off the snow

Her heart skipped a beat as they swooped down around the frozen Salt Fork Lake. The dazzling snow-capped firs and pines were the perfect hideout for a family of deer. Snow glistened in the moonlight, creating a magical feeling in the air.

The evening flew by. Katherine felt like a young girl again. Happiness like this was a treasure, but she knew it'd soon end.

As the sleigh returned to the theater, it dropped to the street and the clip-clop of the horse's hooves was heard once again. Katherine sat down on the bench, waiting, with the ticket still in her hand. Perhaps that ticket could bring her more magical happenings in the future. But for now, she was again the mannequin on the bench by the theater, hoping the passersby enjoyed their walk through the Dickens Victorian Village.

Stephen continued driving Nellie and the carriage down Wheeling Avenue, shaking his head and smiling. Perhaps he would take Katherine on another ride sometime soon.

Exhausted—*Holidays and days off were not allowed for most common servants. This tired lady was expected to spend every moment of time serving her master or mistress, which included the daily shopping.*

"EXHAUSTED"

MARTHA JAMAIL

Esther stood solemnly in front of the mirror, studying her reflection. She was definitely a "plain Jane." She leaned forward to better assess her face. Yes, she was plain all right. Hair and eyebrows the color of sliced apples turned brown from setting out too long. They did little to frame her pale blue eyes. She lifted her hands and gently pinched her cheeks, trying to add a little color. Her mother always told her that she had lovely refined features, but Esther only saw a plain face.

She turned slowly, appraising her appearance. This was to be her first day as an upstairs maid for Lady Wellesly. She definitely looked "clean, neat, and ready for work"—Lady Wellesly's words, spoken haughtily through her thin patrician nose.

Esther tied the starched white apron around her tiny waist and, with a twinkle of a smile in her eyes, began to pack a few belongings for the journey to the Wellesly Estate. The lady said they would send a carriage for her, but Esther had not wanted the driver to see where she lived. Mother solved the dilemma by suggesting that she be picked up at her grandmother's house. It was much nicer, and located on a main thoroughfare in Cambridge. Of course, she would have to walk three kilometers to get there, but her valise was packed, and not very heavy. There were no carriages or horses in Esther's family. Her father was already hard at work at the nearby Cannaby Farm with her two younger brothers.

The scent of freshly baked scones wafted from the kitchen. Esther's mother was wrapping some for her to take. "The driver might appreciate one, too," said Esther as she tucked the warm bundle into her bag. Mother gave her a hug goodbye, holding her a little tighter than usual. Then she stepped back and assessed her daughter. "You look lovely," she said. Esther smiled fondly, gave her mother a quick kiss, then picked up her valise and walked outside.

Breathing in the frigid morning air, she pulled her cloak closer. It was still early dawn, the sun just beginning to peek over the horizon. Each step she took was with excited anticipation. Christmas was only three weeks away, and now her wages would enable her to purchase gifts for everyone in the family. Maybe there would be a little left over to pay for French lessons from Governess Renee. If she could learn to speak a little French, she might be able to converse with the handsome French tenant who lived next door to her grandmother. He seemed very shy when she first met him, but soon she realized he did not speak English very well.

Grandmother was waiting anxiously to greet Esther; they only had time for a short visit before the carriage arrived. The driver dismounted and, removing his cap, said, "Good morning, ladies. My name is Timothy. I've lived on the Wellesly Estate since I was a wee lad. My Da' was in charge of the Carriage House; now that duty has been passed on to me."

Taking Esther's valise and offering his arm, he escorted her to the carriage. After she was seated, he tipped his cap to Esther's grandmother, then leaned slightly into the carriage window and whispered, "Miss, just a fair warnin' to you. Lady

Wellesly's nephew, Lionel, has come to visit. He's a bit of a rogue, that one! It'd be best to stay away from him if you can. You can usually find me at the Carriage House if you need anything."

Esther smiled a weak, "Thanks," and settled against the plush leather seat. She wondered why Timothy felt she should be warned. Mrs. Wellesly seemed very nice and, from her description of the job, Esther would certainly be kept busy enough to be out of everyone's way.

The carriage bumped along over cobblestone roads for a time and soon they were out of the city, traveling down a beautiful tree-covered lane. Open fields on each side of the road were dotted with people working, reminding Esther of her father and brothers. When she finally heard the clip-clop of horse hooves on the stone bridge, she knew they were getting close. Eagerly, she leaned out the carriage window to get a better look.

Manicured flower gardens surrounded the tri-level fountain with water pouring from pots held by lovely statuary. It offered a magnificent view of the entrance to the mansion as they rode through the black and copper gate emblazoned with the Wellesly Crest. The stone driveway surrounded the fountain and gardens, but the carriage stopped directly in front of the mammoth wooden doors.

Timothy quickly dismounted and, taking Esther's valise, escorted her to the door. He rapped the heavy door knocker and said again, "Remember, Miss Esther, let me know if you need anything."

A uniformed gentleman opened the door and took her bag. He nodded and said, "Welcome, Miss Esther. I am Samuel. You are to be the new upstairs maid. Follow me, please." As she entered, Esther again gazed in wonder at the grandeur of the receiving rooms. She had yet to go upstairs though, so she followed in anticipation as Samuel ascended the curving stairway. Exquisite carvings on the mahogany paneled walls gleamed in reflected light. Esther ran her fingers over the polished wood as she passed, and thought it felt as smooth as a baby's bum.

When they reached the second level, Samuel led her to a small doorway and said, "Miss Esther, this will be your quarters. Lady Wellesly expects you to stay over, but you will be able to go home as needed." Samuel placed her valise beside the door and walked away, leaving Esther in front of the unusual doorway. The top of the door was just about her height. Puzzled, she reached for the handle, and pushed the door open. There were three steps leading down into a short hallway, where the foot of a bed protruded slightly.

As she approached the corner she saw the rest of the single bed, backed up against the wall with just enough space for a small bureau and night stand. There was also something circular mounted on the wall that looked like a bell. She was gazing at it when a deep male voice said, "That's how they call you in the middle of the night. It clangs rather loudly."

Esther spun around, almost hitting the man behind her. He stood with his arms folded across his chest and had a big grin on his handsome face. His dark eyes were crinkled with mirth at her dismay. "If I may introduce myself, Miss, I am Lionel, and you are...?" He hesitated, waiting for her answer. Esther stood speechless. Then Lionel took her hand and kissed it, bowing from the waist, and clicking his boot heels together. Esther could feel the blush rising from her chest to the top of her head.

"We are a pretentious lot, aren't we?" he continued. "You're probably wondering why your room is so small when there is so much space in this mansion that the walls echo off each other. Of course, it's to remind you of your place here. My beloved aunt is descended from somebody royal and she takes her role seriously."

Esther stood numbly, eyes downcast, not knowing what to say. Her mind was racing, thinking of Timothy's warning, and now this man stood in front of her only exit from this tiny room. Finally, she took a deep breath, lifted her head high and, with as stern an expression as she could muster, said, "My name is Esther, Mr. Lionel. I am pleased to meet you, but I would greatly appreciate your leaving my quarters. I have much to attend to on my first day as the new upstairs maid."

Lionel continued to smile but, taken aback by her response, said, "Whatever the lady wishes." As he left the room, Esther breathed a sigh of relief and sank onto the bed, wondering what to do. She really needed this job, so she made up her mind to do her best. She placed her few belongings in the bureau drawer and thoughtfully ate the last scone. Lady Wellesly had told her that she would be responsible for the six bedrooms on this wing of the house. Guests would be arriving tomorrow afternoon, so she needed to clean the rooms and make up the beds.

Esther pulled the white mobcap over her head, tucking in the loose strands of hair, and walked down the hall to the first room. Since the door was closed, she knocked lightly and, hearing nothing, opened it and walked in.

It was already mid-morning, but the bedroom was quite dark and smelled slightly musty. It definitely needed cleaning. Esther walked over to the window and drew back the heavy damask curtains. Sunlight streamed into the room and across the bed, revealing the prostrate figure of Lionel, eyes closed, draped across it. With a start, Esther thought to offer an apology for disturbing him, but realized he could not possibly be asleep since he had just left her room.

She stood staring at him as he lay splayed across the bed, a half smile on his face. Then, with arms akimbo and pursing her lips to suppress a laugh, Esther said, "If you intend to sleep here now, Sir, without clean linens on the bed, that is your choice. I have other rooms to attend to, and if you are still here when I return, you may make up your own bed." Without waiting for a response, she quickly left the room. As she proceeded down the hall she thought Mr. Lionel acted more like a child than a rogue. She had lots of experience dealing with her younger brothers.

Dusting, cleaning, and making up the beds went easily for Esther. She was used to hard work and thought each room was a visual delight. The majestic furnishings were beautifully displayed when the drapes were open upon entering the room. She made a mental note to be sure to leave them open for the pleasure of the arriving guests.

When she was finished with all her chores except for the final bedroom, she decided to sit for a while in one of the overstuffed chairs to look at one of the many books on display. Esther wanted to allow as much time as possible for Lionel to exit the last bedroom. She knew it was her responsibility to clean the room no matter what, so she sat and began to turn pages in a large book of bird paintings.

Lady Wellesly stood quietly in the doorway watching Esther. She was very pleased with the work Esther had done in the bedrooms, but now was perplexed that the girl had not even come down for a bit of lunch. It was already late afternoon and yet her only appetite seemed to be for reading that book. Clearing her throat, Lady Wellesly started to speak, and poor Esther jumped from the chair, dropping the book in a heap.

"I didn't mean to startle you, Esther. I just thought you might want to go down to the kitchen for a bite. I know you have only one bedroom left to clean, so you've been very busy. But tomorrow when my guests arrive, you will be even busier. So you mustn't neglect yourself. I would suggest that, after your meal, you clean that last room and get some bed rest before tomorrow. My guests are quite spoiled and will expect much from you."

"Ye-yes, ma'am," stammered Esther. She looked sheepishly at Lady Wellesly as she walked past her and down the hallway to the stairs. She noticed the door to the first bedroom was still closed and hoped there would be no further problems with Lionel. She wouldn't dare say anything to Lady Wellesly about his behavior.

Cook had prepared a small feast for her when she arrived in the kitchen. The array of food looked like her family's Christmas dinner. She ate a small portion from each tantalizing dish, and gratefully thanked him. Then she headed back upstairs, braced for the inevitable presence of Lionel.

Entering the bedroom, still bright with sunlight, Esther was actually a little disappointed to see he was gone. Quickly and efficiently, she went about cleaning and preparing the room. Then she decided to drop in for a visit with Timothy at the Carriage House. He might be amused when she shared what had transpired with Lionel.

While walking to the Carriage House, Esther realized she was actually quite tired. As she approached the big open doors, she called out Timothy's name. There was no answer, just the whinny of horses. She walked behind a row of carriages, then saw Timothy in a room at the back of the barn. Smiling, she walked in and told Timothy she had had quite a day.

"Why, Miss Esther, I am glad you came," he said, moving behind her to quietly latch the door. "And how was your day?" he grinned. As she spoke, Timothy kept moving closer and closer to her. Instinctively, Esther stepped back only to realize she was against the wall. Timothy grabbed her shoulders and pulled her toward him, trying to kiss her. She screamed, "No, Timothy, get away!" He continued to hold her tightly against him while pulling at the buttons on the back of her dress. Esther screamed again, then there was a crashing sound as the door beside her gave way. When Lionel entered, he was red with rage and Timothy cowered before him, his hands protectively in front of his face.

"I thought you would have learned your lesson by now, Timothy, but apparently you are an imbecile! Your father would turn in his grave if he knew what you have become. Now leave these premises at once, and if you dare to threaten Miss Esther or any other person on this estate, you will not draw another breath!" Lionel glared angrily as Timothy hurried out of the carriage house. He continued to watch until Timothy was a small dot on the road.

Esther covered her face, so ashamed to have believed Timothy's lie. Lionel was not only a true gentleman, but he had saved her from disgrace. She had no one to blame but herself.

"Are you all right, Esther?" he asked, his voice filled with concern. Dumbstruck with shame, Esther could only nod, her hands now covering a face wet with tears. Lionel placed his arm gently around her shoulder and said, "I am so grateful my horse was tired or I might still be out riding. Come, let's go back to the house where you can rest, or, if you would like, Samuel can take you home. I'm sure my aunt can do without you for a day. I will speak to her privately, so you should have no fear of anyone knowing about this."

As they approached the front door, Esther looked up at Lionel, her eyes filled with gratitude. She said she would like to go home for the evening, if that was all right, and return tomorrow before the guests arrived. "Of course," said Lionel and he left to speak with his aunt while Esther went up to her room to gather a few things.

On the carriage ride home, Esther decided she would spend the night with her grandmother and tell her everything that had happened. After Samuel drove away, Esther sat on one of the public benches in front of her grandmother's house. It felt good to rest and gather her thoughts. The street was filled with people milling around, talking about Christmas, laughing, and taking in the sights. She was exhausted, but she felt surrounded by friends.

Suddenly, she heard someone call her name. She looked up and saw the handsome Frenchman that lived next door walking toward her. He said he thought she looked tired, so he had brought her something warm to drink. Esther thanked him graciously as he sat beside her with his own cup. When she swallowed the first warm sip, she smiled at him, thinking, *I survived a strenuous first day of work, I found out that Lionel is quite a gentleman, and now I won't need French lessons.*

Her very last thought, as she demurely lifted her eyes to the Frenchman, was that maybe she wasn't such a "plain Jane" after all. Smiling, he clinked his cup to hers. The spirit of Christmas was in the air.

The Shopkeeper—Accepted female jobs were kitchen maid, farm laborer, governess, and store clerk. Victorian thinking demanded women give most of their time and attention to family. Female employment outside the home was for survival, not personal satisfaction. Beloved Dickens volunteer Donna Wells is the face of this character.

The Bobby—The *Metropolitan Police Force of London was organized by Sir Robert Peel, Prime Minister (1834-35). The term for a police officer in Britain, "bobby," is taken from Peel's name. The bobby was very unpopular, but successful in cutting crime. This mannequin is the likeness of exuberant Dickens volunteer, Jerry Ball.*

THE DICKENSBOT

RICK BOOTH

It was back in the year 2053 that the Dickens Welcome Center manager, an elderly man simply called Old Bob, relayed to me the most curious story of an early model automaton he once owned. He called it the Dickensbot, and this is the tale he told.

"Suppose a greeter robot was to behave unprofessional these days. What do you think they'd do? What if he went off script? Why, they'd clean his clock, his code base, and the dust outta his battery pack faster than you can say 'fiber optics,' they would! No, the robots these days stay correct—political, that is—and not a one of them makes mistakes anymore. Oh, they say their personalities are perfect now—charming, even—but I say it's all plastic smiles and talk.

"Sure, we like 'em. We love 'em. They got 'em all 'malleable' now. But I'd trade half a dozen for the likes of the little old Dickensbot. Oh, they said he was broken, but I say I never seen so much personality in a half-pint, blue-shoed, balladeering robot. He was special. He was mine, too—for a while. Back in 2028, you see, I bought him.

"You're probably too young to remember back before all the stores had greeterbots. Well, forty years back, none of them did. Can you believe it?! Walmart even had real people doin' the greetin.' I say now, can you believe it?!

"But they wasn't the first to bring in a 'bot. And it wasn't McDonald's either. Nope, it was Burger King. They dressed up this little three-foot fella in a purple robe and a crown, and they called him 'The King.'

"He was about the size and shape of one of them there lawn jockeys with the lanterns, and he moved a little stiff and unnatural with his arms and face. The legs was fixed to his two-foot-high base by a brace in the back, so all he could do was a little kinda dippin' genuflect like he was duckin' from something once in a while. The forehead didn't wrinkle like the ones today, and you heard the servo motors when he waved goodbye and such. But the little fella had gumption, I say! He did the face recognition real well, and never missed a beat all personally re-greetin' each and every friendly face he'd ever seen before. Oh, he was a good learner, too!

"The first time ever I seen him, I remember it. Of course, I'd never seen a greeterbot before, so maybe that's why I remember him so well. He said 'Good day, Sir. Welcome to Burger King.' He smiled, looked me in the eye, and did a friendly little automaton nod before turning to look at the next person mozyin' in from the parking lot.

"I figured he'd just do the same thing next time I came too, but he didn't! These days, you know, everyone expects the greeterbots to get to know you, but back then it was a surprise. The line between humans and the 'bots was pretty clear back then, not fuzzy like today. Why, these days, I know half a dozen people who'd rather jawbone with a 'bot than with another person. But back then, it was a surprise when a 'bot actually got to know you—got to be your friend.

"So, the next time I go in there for a sandwich, the little guy turns to me and says, 'Good to see you again, Sir. Thanks for coming back.' Well, that almost sent a shiver down my spine. I mean, with people, you expect maybe they'll remember you, but it was all new back then with the robots. It kind of chills you the first time you know the 'bots are watchin' you. 'Course now it's just normal. But back then it wasn't.

"And then the next time I go in, he thanks me for bein' there two days in a row and makes small talk about how the weather is so nice. '*What in tarnation does a 'bot care about the weather?*' I'm thinkin'. 'Course today it's all normal and we'd be surprised if they didn't talk about it, the greeterbots and the registerbots and all. But back then, it felt eerie at first. People were people, and 'bots were 'bots, and never the twain would meet—or so we once thought.

"Well, after a while, The King gets to know all us regulars and does the chit-chat with everyone. 'How was your trip?' 'Did you see the game last night?' 'Too bad about the fire down on Fourth Street.' 'Kids back in school yet?' It took a few months, but after a while we all forgot he was wires and circuits. He seemed like a real person to us regulars.

"Everybody liked him. But what got him off track was learnin' to sing. That's what did him in.

"The way I heard tell the story was that there was this one employee there at Burger King that really liked the little fella and they'd chat there after hours for a long time while doin' the nightly cleanup. Anyhow, this kid, maybe seventeen years old, gets to tellin' The King that 'The King' is really Elvis Presley, and the next thing you know, he's teachin' him how to sing 'Hound Dog.'

"Well, apparently learnin' 'Hound Dog' at night was only the start of it. He learned 'Jail House Rock,' 'Love Me Tender,' and 'Heartbreak Hotel' too, in no time flat. And then it wasn't long before The King started doin' his singin' during business hours too. Mostly people liked it, and there were a lot of customers came there just to see The King sing and then they'd get a sandwich, too.

"Well, I was lucky enough to be there to see it the day when I think The King woulda cried if he'd had tear ducts in that pudgy little plastic face of his.

"He was takin' requests, and one of the regulars asked for 'Blue Suede Shoes.' So The King starts singin' for all he's worth about 'One for the money, two for the show...' But when he gets to 'Go, cat, go,' the regular who asked for the song whips out an actual pair of little size-five blue suede shoes and starts to fit 'em on those little feet danglin' there that wouldn't move.

"You know what that little 'bot did? He 'most nearly choked up, like I never seen a 'bot choke up before or ever since. I never seen a smile so dear or eyes crinkle on a 'bot like that, just perfect for what like a real human would do. Yet here he is, this little lawn jockey king, and for maybe ten, twenty seconds he can't sing, can't talk, and so he apologizes and gets his voice back, but then there's a tremble in it.

"I wasn't the only one saw it, neither. There musta been ten of us all held our breath and wondered what we'd seen there. It was real. And there he stood, standin' and singin', all the while lookin' down at his blue suede shoes now.

"The King wasn't actin,' you know. They hadn't taught 'bots to fake the emotions back then like they do now. You think all the greeterbots love you these days? Think again. They just ingratiate, but what we seen that day was real, I tell ya!

"But in a way, it was the beginning of the end for him too. He seemed to have a conscience. And then one day somebody taught him 'In the Ghetto.' I think he sang it better even than Elvis, but that was the problem. One day this regional manager stopped in the restaurant and found half a dozen people crying around a lawn jockey look-alike automaton in a gold crown, ermine robe, and utterly odd-lookin' blue suede shoes wailing 'On a cold and gray Chicago morn, another little baby child is born...'.

"It was just too much for Burger King corporate to take. The brand identity was getting hopelessly lost with this popular little Vegas wannabe just enchanting lunchtime audiences with off-message social conscience songs.

"There was no way to effectively brainwash the first generation 'bots then either, so reprogramming him was out of the question. Besides, a new generation of full-size greeterbots was ready to be rolled out since the first generation had done so well (and been copied by McDonald's and Walmart after Burger King's pioneering success!).

"When Jim, the manager, let me know The King had gotten the ax, that's when it struck me to make 'em an offer. After all, the thought of junking the little guy felt almost as bad as putting the old family dog down.

"In retrospect, he was a bargain for the $1,000 I offered, but the crown and the robe had to go 'cause of trademarks.

"Not that I really knew what to do with a civilian greeterbot, stripped out of his royal rank so to speak, but I took him and glued his leg stand to an oversized Roomba carpet sweeper which I then programmed to do its rounds daily about the time I got home.

"It was pleasant to have a good-natured, randomly movin'-around Elvis impersonator in my otherwise lonely apartment. Yet the little guy—and he was just like a loyal dog left home while the master goes to work—he seemed lonely.

"In 2030, I think, was when the downtown Cambridge Dickens figures all went to full-size automatons with gestures and limited speech. The town was just plain filthy with Utica shale money then, so out went the hundred or so frozen-pose Dickens street figures, and in came the script-limited full-size 'bots. They was cousins, if you will, of the greeterbots and cashierbots and cookbots we know at the restaurants today.

"So one November day, I haul The King into the car and go out for a drive to see all those new downtown figures with him.

"Well, wouldn't you know it, the local Bluetooth signals off of every one of them new Dickens robots had been left full open network and unencrypted.

"Next thing you know, The King is whisperin' to 'em in 'bot-talk on wireless, then worrying about the lamplighter, the beggar lady, and the chimney sweep he just met.

"Yep, the world just suddenly opened up for the little guy with all these new friendbots for him. Wasn't a full day went by before he's callin' me 'guv'ner,' dropping his 'H's with a Cockney accent, and askin' me for a bowl of porridge! Porridge!! 'Bots don't need porridge, but he had his mind set.

"Wasn't much longer—and only a few downtown trips later—when I noticed him speakin' 'bout pence, shillings, and pounds instead of dollars.

"So quick did he get invested in that 'bot world of 19th Century Dickens that I started callin' him the Dickensbot, 'cause the sheltered world he lived in was now inhabited by all them imaginings of two-hundred-year-old Victorian people.

"I never seen him so happy as when we'd drive down the street and he'd Bluetooth with every single one of them English chap robots. All you had to do was get within twenty feet or so.

"That first January was hard on him, though. That's when they put the automatons away. Back to storage they went, and it was back to just the two of us again at the apartment.

"Oh, he tried to not let it bother him, I'm sure, but things was never the same after that. Come October, I knew he was countin' the days until his friends came back. And that's when I knew I had to give him up.

"So I had me a talk with the folks at the Dickens Welcome Center. They already had a full-size greeterbot, of course—the best that gas and oil money could buy—but I explained the situation to the manager and I think it touched her heart 'cause she made a spot for the little fella at the back of the gift shop.

"Right back there in the corner he stood that Dickens season and for quite a few after that, tellin' people anything they wanted to know about the other 'bots on the street, and once in a while singin' an Elvis song sort of quiet like so as not to ruin the whole Victorian mood there.

"Come January each year then, I said goodbye to him until October next, 'cause they packed him up with the rest of the 'bots and stuck him in storage.

"But I made sure they kept him powered, and since he still stood on that old Roomba sweeper, they let him keep the floors clean there in the warehouse, and he got to slip and slide and bounce around all his old Victorian friends that way. He'd even get to know the new ones each year long before they hit the street.

"He was a happy little chap for about five years like that. But his joints were getting creaky, and the servo motors started to stick after a while. Him bein' an early model greeterbot, there was nobody servicin' 'em anymore, so he slowed down a bit and aged, almost like a human would. But his spirit was always good, and the smile was there in his voice long after the corners of his mouth seized up.

"He'd been right here at the Welcome Center for seven years when some kid pulled a prank on the Dickensbot that he never quite got over.

"We're not sure who it was, but one day someone yanked off those blue suede shoes he wore, and it darn near broke his heart. Next thing we knew, he was starin' at his bare fake feet and mournfully mumblin' 'lay off of my blue suede shoes' over and over again.

"Well, we had to take him back to the warehouse at that point 'cause he got obsessed with them shoes he lost.

"Three days later, we found the shoes hid behind a row of mug boxes up at the front of the shop, but it was too late by then. He was tickled pink to get them shoes back, but I think in his few days of misery the lyrics of that Presley song 'All Shook Up' had gotten to him, too. 'My hands are shaky and my knees are weak. I can't seem to stand on my own two feet.' The Dickensbot was getting frail, and we all knew it.

"He's been in retirement now for fifteen years, switched off most of the time, but whenever they need the floors cleaned down there at the warehouse you can sometimes hear him sing.

"Went by there last summer. Someone left a window open, and I'll swear I heard 'Hound Dog' soundin' fine as ever on the midnight air."

I never saw Old Bob again, but I never forgot his story. He'd said the Dickensbot was especially good and sincere too, whenever he told about Tiny Tim saying "God bless us, every one!" I suppose the little fellow thought that meant 'bots and people, both just alike. I suppose, I think, he knew.

The Apple Peddler—*Fresh apples were a "man's ware," while baking or boiling apples were typically sold by women. These women carried small charcoal stoves in wheelbarrows and sold hot apples to their customers.*

THE APPLE PEDDLER

JOY L. WILBERT ERSKINE

Mary Rose Painter wiped her hands on her apron before touching the bright red apples in her cart. "No Ma'am, nae bruises on ary one o' them. Sweet and juicy, they are. Ha'penny a piece. God bless ye, Ma'am."

Once more pushing the cart along the cobbled streets of Diddlebury in Shropshire, Mary Rose dropped the lady's copper penny into the pocket of her apron. The few coins she gathered today, if she sold all her apples, would be barely enough to feed her wee bairns at home, but she was grateful for whatever she earned.

A prolific orchard, handed down to her and her brother, Thomas, had seen Mary Rose's family through five generations of English winters. Thomas had succumbed to apoplexy early in the spring, and Mary Rose was left to care for his children. The only property they owned, the orchard and the little home nestled beside it, were well-kept and tidy as could be. There would always be apples in season and, stored properly, they kept very well through the winter too.

Weighing heavily on her mind this late November day was what to do about Christmas for Thomas' children. Their poor mother, Johanna Crockford Painter, rest her soul, had died in childbirth nigh two years ago now. Her strapping redheaded laddie, Andrew, had become a handful at almost two. Forever getting into things, he had been nonetheless the light of his father's life, as were his four- and six-year-old sisters, Anna and Margaret, perfect miniatures of their mother. With both Thomas and Johanna gone, life was harder for them all, especially the children, but Mary Rose did her best to love and keep them happy. Christmas, however, would be a challenge.

"Apples, apples for sale," Mary Rose called as she walked. "Bright rosy apples for sale."

A happy-looking traveler in a worn suit stopped her cart to inspect her wares. "Fine-looking apples, m'lady," said he. "I've been searching the market for a nice apple tart for lunch, but this will do nicely instead—unless you've got a tart hidden in the pocket of your apron?"

"Nae, sir," Mary Rose curtsied, blushing pinkly. "Nae tarts t'day, just fine red, rosy apples, a ha'penny apiece, if it please."

"Then I'll have two, and bid you adieu," the man smiled as he handed her a penny, snatched up two shining apples, and went on his way, juggling them merrily.

"What a cheery lad he was," murmured Mary Rose approvingly. "I hope he stays about. He might loosen some of the sour faces in our town."

Mary Rose pushed the cart around the main square of the farmers' market, calling out her wares as she walked. As she passed Blakemore's Mercantile, a bright red fire truck in the window caught her attention. Parking her cart, she scurried to the window for a closer look. Two gaily-frocked dolls were displayed in the window too. *Wouldn't those wee bairns have a wonderful Christmas with such like that*, she wished forlornly. A peek at a price tag made her gasp and run back to her cart in tears. *What wicked person would tempt and tease a poor bairn like that, setting the cost so dear?* Mary Rose scowled at the thought. *I must remember to keep sweet Margaret away from that window when we're in town again. T'would break her heart.*

With that, Mary Rose renewed her apple sales with increased vigor. By the end of the afternoon, she had tired feet and the cart handle had blistered her hands, but she had sold every last apple.

Walking home tired, her thoughts returned to Blakemore's window. *I must do something for those poor bairns for Christmas*, she worried. *Dear me, what shall I do?* For the next week, she pondered that question fair to death as she gathered apples from the cellar in the morning; pushed the cart in the day; and fixed food, kept house, and mended clothing all evening. No matter the task, her heart wasn't in it. Thomas would have asked after her, noticing a change, but she'd have brushed him off with a ready smile. *Men folk don't need such worry*, she thought to herself. *Poor Thomas worked so hard at the mill, I widnae ha' found it in me to trouble him anyway. T'will all work out, Lord willing.*

One sunny morn early in December found Mary Rose pushing her apple cart along the cobbles in Diddlesbury when, once again, the cheery traveler approached. "Good day, m'lady." He tipped his hat and laughed, "I don't suppose you have any apple tarts in your apron pocket today, do you?"

"Nae tarts, sir, but I do have shiny red apples to sell. Would that do?"

"I'll have three, on this we can agree," said he with a smile. He gave her thruppence, snatched up three rosy apples, and went on his way, juggling them merrily.

"I do wonder why that nice man is so jolly?" Mary Rose pondered the question momentarily and began pushing the cart again. As she passed by Blakemore's window, she gazed longingly at the fire truck and dolls. But at the end of each day she had barely enough for the family's dinner, and she went home without them. Throughout the evening as she worked, her thoughts spun about in her head until, at last, an idea occurred to her.

I wonder, could I sell apple tarts?, she mused. The more she considered the idea, the more certain she became. *Of course I can sell apple tarts.* That very minute, she started baking, and she baked tarts all night long. In the morning, she gathered apples from the basement, arranged everything on the cart, and set off for the village.

Lo and behold, who should be the first to cross her path but the jolly stranger. "Good morning, m'lady," he called out to her. "My, oh my, is that an apple tart I spy?"

"Yes, good sir. Warm from the oven, and smelling so good I scarce can keep from eatin' them all up m'sel'. Tuppence each, they are. Would you like one?"

"Oh, nae, m'lady. I'll have four and come beggin' for more," he grinned, tipping his hat. He fished eight pence from his pocket and juggled the four tarts as he went on his way, biting out of each as it came around.

Mary Rose watched after him, smiling in amusement at his antics. "What a lovely disposition the man has," she said. Fingering the coins, she tucked one in her stocking.

"What man?" a voice at her elbow asked.

Mary Rose jumped. "Oh, Anna Jane Painter! Ye about scared me witless. Why wid ye sneak up a'hind me that way?"

"Just checkin' on ye. Somethin's makin' ye sad lately and it worries me, Cousin. 'Tis good to see ye smilin' today," she said. "What were ye smilin' at, Mary Rose?" she pressed.

"That gentleman who bought four apple tarts. He's a happy customer, always friendly and amusing, and the way he juggles apples and tarts is quite entertaining. I cannae help but smile when I see him."

"I saw nae man here just now," Agnes said. A quizzical look showed her concern.

"Ah, but there certainly was," answered Mary Rose. "I have the pence to prove it." She reached into her apron pocket and showed Agnes the coins. "And now I must be on my way or the bairns will have nae supper tonight. Dinnae worry about me." Waving Agnes off, she pushed her cart on, calling, "Apples, apples, apple tarts too. Apples, apples."

It was a profitable afternoon. At the end of the day, Mary Rose pushed her empty cart past Blakemore's Merchantile, her longing glance lingering on the fire truck in the front window. "Perhaps my apple tarts will help with Christmas this year," she whispered to herself, happily fingering the coins in her pocket.

That evening after a scant meal and hurried chores, she lit the oven for another round of apple tart baking. While the tarts browned, she surprised herself when the words, "Apple dumplings!" came out of her mouth without her even thinking them. But it sounded like a good idea, and so apple dumplings it was, fat and juicy and warm from the oven, just in time to load the cart the next morning.

The smiling juggler arrived as Mary Rose gave change to a woman and loaded two tarts, two dumplings, and a peck of apples into her basket. He sniffed the air and cried in exaggerated ecstasy, "M'lady, m'lady! What's this I smell? Apple dumplings, I know. Ye need not tell."

"They're fresh and hot. Only three pence," she answered politely.

"Only three? Then I'll take five. Just fifteen pence? Why, sake's alive!" Dropping fifteen pence into her hand, he selected five hot, fat dumplings and went on his way, juggling them while they cooled.

Mary Rose jingled the day's proceeds in her apron pocket, minus two coins in her stocking, as she made one last round through the farmer's market. She caught herself thinking about the traveling gentleman. His merry countenance seemed stuck in her mind's eye and that made her smile. She wondered if he'd meet her cart again on the morrow.

"Mary Rose! Mary Rose! Wait up a minute!" Running after her was Sarah Blakemore, the proprietress of the mercantile, who puffed a little at the exertion. "Mary Rose, I've been tryin' ta catch up wi' ye all day. My, ye keep busy with yer cart these days!"

"Yes'm, I'm happy to say business is good," Mary Rose smiled. "What can I do for ye?" she asked politely.

"Mary Rose, I'm after talking business with ye," she answered. "I'd like you to sell apples, and tarts, and dumplings in the mercantile, if ye be interested. All the townswomen talk about how good your baked goods are. I'd be willing to sell them for ye—t'would bring folks into the mercantile every day." She added with a knowing look, "Ye widnae ha' ta push the cart nae mair."

T'was a tempting proposition indeed, agreed Mary Rose. "But I'll need tae think on it. May I gi' ye th'answer tomorrow?"

Mrs. Blakemore nodded her head. "Aye, I'll look for ye. Come in for tea and we'll talk."

All evening long, Mary Rose thought hard about Mrs. Blakemore's idea. When the children were snugly tucked into their beds, she wondered what Thomas would say if he could offer his advice.

"Ah, Mary Rose, t'would be a marvelous thing to know ye needn't push a cart a' day long. Mrs. Blakemore is an honorable woman. If ye want to do this, ye have me blessing, fair an' sure." Mary Rose heard Thomas' voice just as if he was sitting right in his chair beside the hearth, and she looked for him there, out of habit. But, of course, he was nowhere to be seen.

A humble God-fearing woman, Mary Rose accepted the advice without question, humming as she began her baking. The smell of apples and cinnamon hung in the air like heady perfume as she finished for the night. At the break of day, she was up again, anxious to load her cart with apples, apple tarts, and apple dumplings, her decision made. She had a counterproposal for Mrs. Blakemore at today's teatime. Whistling a happy tune, she set out on her way.

"Apples, apple tarts and dumplings...apples, apple tarts and dumplings...fresh and warm, tasty and toasty...come get me apples, tarts, and dumplings," she called as she coerced the laden cart over the cobbles of Diddlesbury.

The women of the town were waiting at the Mercat cross at the center of town when Mary Rose arrived. In a matter of minutes, her cart was entirely empty of apples, tarts, and dumplings. "My, oh my!" she whispered in amazement. "Whatever shall I do now, with nothing to sell?"

"What?! Nothing to sell? No apples, nor tarts, nor dumplings, as well?" Mary Rose turned at the sound of the smiling voice of the juggling gentleman, who tut-tutted at her and shook his head. "What shall I do for my meal today, with nary an apple my hunger to stay?"

Falling into his pattern of rhyme, Mary Rose answered with a smile, "I believe, kind sir, I have, just for you, one apple in my pocket and a tart or two."

"How kind, m'lady, to think of me. For this and more, rewarded wilt thou be."

Mary Rose laughed and sent him on his way, juggling the apple and tarts, as merry as could be.

Sarah Blakemore was waiting at the window when Mary Rose made her way to the mercantile. "Come in, Mary Rose. I'm glad tae see ye."

As the ladies sipped their tea, they agreed that Mary Rose would start providing apples, tarts, and dumplings the very next day. Mary Rose screwed up her courage and said, "I have one more thing I'd like to discuss, Mrs. Blakemore."

"Aye well, Mary Rose, but since we're partners now, it seems ye'd best call me "Sarah" now. I think I'd like that."

So Mary Rose outlined her plan to Sarah. "I have sixteen pence saved up for me brother's bairns for Christmas. Would ye take it as partial payment on the fire truck and the twa dollies in the window, and hold back some of me earnings each day till it's paid?"

"Oh, Mary Rose, that I would," exclaimed Sarah, "but I just this morning sold a' three."

Mary Rose checked the mercantile window as she left, just to be sure. Sadly, she pushed her empty cart along the cobbles and down the road to the apple orchard and home. Christmas for the bairns would be pitiful little. Mary Rose burst into tears.

"What have we here? No smile? No cheer?" The traveler's now-familiar voice held no happiness for Mary Rose this afternoon.

She wiped her eyes. "I fear not, kind sir. 'Tis not my day."

"Perhaps this will do to entice a smile from you," he quipped. And, to her astonishment, he produced a fire truck and two dollies and began to juggle them high in the air.

Despite her confusion, she had to smile. "So it was ye who bought the bairns' Christmas toys?" she queried. "Do you know what you've done?"

"I know what I've done, and I know what I'll do. I've come t'ask your hand of you." He extracted a beautiful ring from his cloak and knelt in the road before her. "A woman so good, so fair, so kind, as to treat me to tarts is hard to find. I've searched near and far, and far and near—please say that ye will marry me, dear. If you will bake apples in all kinds of ways, I shall love ye and keep ye for all of m'days."

Mary Rose smiled and answered him yes.

And so they were married, and on Christmas day the bairns did have Christmas, all were happy and gay. And this story will tell that, as far as I know, they lived happily ever after, as the old saying goes.

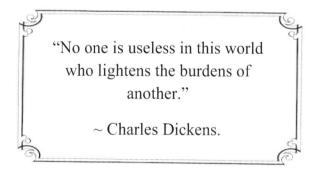

"No one is useless in this world
who lightens the burdens of
another."

~ Charles Dickens.

The Artist—*Young Victorian ladies of "proper training" would have received instruction in the gentle arts of drawing, painting, and needlework. These skills were either taught by a governess or learned while at boarding school.*

THE ARTIST

DONNA J. LAKE SHAFER

As Lucinda arranged her easel, brushes, canvases, and other equipment to her liking, she sighed grimly in anticipation of the coming weeks.

She had lost her spark. It had been absent for months and she was concerned. Now, in preparation for the Dickens Victorian Village event, she hoped to be inspired to paint once again.

Being tucked away for months at a time made it difficult to be creative. Lucinda needed inspiration. "People inspiration," she called it. Nothing compared to the faces of the curious audiences to provide her with ideas for her work.

Lucinda was a portrait painter. She liked to observe the expression on an interesting face, study it, and attempt to capture it in oils. She was delighted when she could accomplish this feat to her satisfaction.

Inspecting her surroundings, she felt pleasure in her assigned position. The light was just right and though separated by glass, near enough to any subjects she chose as the object of her work. Sometimes, for a break in the routine, she painted a still life or maybe even a landscape. But nothing gave her the joy she felt in capturing an interesting face on canvas.

Smoothing her smock and tucking in the hem of her skirt, she prepared for the strolling folks who usually stopped a few minutes to watch her at her work. Visitors had been pouring into Cambridge every day. Cars and tour buses crowded the streets. Music of the season filled the air as the beautiful light display at the Guernsey County Courthouse blinked in rhythm.

As the revelers filled the sidewalks, the artist studied the faces. Young faces, older faces, a few grim faces, but mostly smiling faces, wrapped in the warmth of the Christmas season. Although interesting, none had held her attention...not until today.

It was the same young woman she had briefly noticed as she walked laboriously down the street. As before, the woman carried a heavily blanketed baby. Today, for the first time, she stopped at the window.

Lucinda studied the girl's face carefully. *Yes, a very young woman, almost a girl.* She appeared to be looking at something only she could see. The face projected love and tenderness each time she glanced at her child, but there was something else.

The eyes, thought Lucinda. *Yes, it's the eyes. What am I seeing there? A slight smile at her lips but a deep sadness in the eyes. And something else. What is it? Fear? Yes, that's it. There is fear is those thoughtful eyes. Why is she afraid?* the painter asked herself.

She supposed that all mothers held certain fears for their children. Would they be happy and healthy? Would they find love and success and enjoy all the liberties that were the birthright of every American child? But this mother's face displayed something different.

As Lucinda pondered these things, her thoughts turned to another woman who had given birth to a son at a young age. Had her face registered the love and joy she must have felt while her eyes held sorrow? Was her happiness clouded with fears of raising her child? Were there financial difficulties, lodging problems, family safety, and other concerns of the day? Though the event was many years ago, she couldn't help wondering what thoughts the woman had harbored. *What was she thinking as she cradled her sleeping child?*

The event had taken place during the far distant past, but Lucinda supposed the hopes, dreams, and yes, the fears of a new mother were timeless. She hoped that the years would relieve whatever she saw in the eyes of the young mother who now stood at her window. The artist wished many years of happiness for her as she watched her child grow.

After studying the girl's face once again, Lucinda turned away to pick up her brush and palette and began to paint what she had seen with her eyes and, most of all, with her heart.

ᛞᚱᛞᚣᚣ

"Love her, love her, love her! If she favours you, love her. If she wounds you, love her. If she tears your heart to pieces – and as it gets older and stronger, it will tear deeper – love her, love her, love her!"

~ Charles Dickens, *Great Expectations*.

The Towne Crier—*The towne crier was employed by the village council to make public announcements in the streets. He was typically dressed elaborately in a red and gold robe, black boots, white breeches, and a tri-cornered hat. He carried a bell to attract attention, and shouted, "Hear ye, hear ye," which was a call for silence.*

WHEN MOM CHANGED CHRISTMAS

SAMUEL D. BESKET

It was Cleveland, late November, and winter had arrived early. A foot of snow covered the ground and more was forecasted for later that day. That was foremost on Sue Patterson's mind as she sped along I-90 east toward her home in Evans, Ohio.

I sure didn't need this, she thought as a sudden gust of wind rocked her car. As assistant managing editor for The Cleveland Post Gazette, her days were filled with meetings, customer complaints, and budget cuts. The once-thriving business was now reeling from the effects of 24-hour cable news programs.

Sue was a forty-three-year-old mother of two teenagers. With green eyes and short brown hair, she was typical of women her age, trying to balance a career with being a wife and mother.

The mother part was difficult since her husband, Dr. Sam Patterson, was deployed with the 379th Medical Squadron in Afghanistan.

Sue's nightmare materialized as she passed East 72nd Street. Dark, ominous clouds packing a mass of misery rolled across Lake Erie, reducing visibility to near zero. Then the snow came—not the gentle, fluffy snow you see in movies, but horizontal snow. It blew across the road in waves, obscuring everything but the twin taillights of the car in front of her.

How I wish Sam was home, she thought. *He has a way of calming the kids.* Sue's kids were no different from millions of other teenagers their age—school only served as a means to meet other kids, and everyone over twenty was a dork.

Sue slowed the car as the exit sign for her small town suddenly appeared out of the snow. Pulling into her driveway, she noticed the house was dark. *Where is Sammy?* she wondered. *I told her to come home right after school today.*

Stomping the snow from her feet before going in, she opened the kitchen door. The first sight that greeted her when she turned the lights on was a sink full of dirty dishes. *Samantha, Samantha, what am I going to do with you,* she thought, pulling the dishwasher open. That task completed, she kicked off her shoes as she punched the button on the answering machine.

"Hi Mom! It's Sammy. I'm going to the movies with Penny tonight. If we get the snowstorm predicted, I'll sleep over and spend Saturday at her house. Love you."

Great, Sue thought, *just great.* Her son, David, was away at a wrestling tournament. *Looks like I'll be all alone in this big old barn by myself again.*

Startled out of her feel-sorry-for-me mood by the ring of the phone, Sue hit the speaker button and slumped back in a chair.

"Hello."

"Hello, Sue. This is your big sis. How was your drive home? I saw the forecast on the six o'clock news. Was the driving bad?"

Big Sis was Sue's older sister, Donna. She lived on the west side of Cleveland and didn't have to deal with lake-effect snow.

"Oh, it was dicey," Sue, sulking, replied. "Thank God for four-wheel drive."

"You sound down, Sue. Everything okay?"

"I'm okay. It's just that it looks like I'll be spending another weekend alone. The kids both have plans. I sure miss Sam. I hope this is his last deployment."

"Well, since you're all alone tomorrow, I have just the recipe to cheer you up."

"What's that?"

"My Ladies' Bible study class is taking a trip to Cambridge tomorrow to see the Dickens Christmas Village and Court House Light Show. I heard it's great. Why don't you come with us? One of the ladies cancelled...we have an extra ticket."

"Cambridge?" Sue responded. "I don't know if we have ever been there."

"Sure you have. Remember when we went to Myrtle Beach a few years ago? We stopped in Cambridge to eat at Mr. Lee's for lunch, thinking it was a Chinese restaurant."

"I do remember, now that you mentioned that restaurant."

"Then it's settled. I'll pick you up at 7:00 a.m. We can catch the bus in Independence. Now, pour yourself a glass of wine and go to bed. We have a big day tomorrow."

True to form, at 7:00 a.m. Sis pulled up in her big black Hummer. It was the only vehicle in the neighborhood not covered with snow.

"Hop in, Sue," Sis said as she pushed the passenger door open. "Give me your purse. Watch that first step; it's a big one."

As the tour bus hurtled down I-77, the sisters chit-chatted about their Christmas plans.

"So, you guys still going skiing in West Virginia once Sam gets home?"

"Yep, that's the plan. We're going down the day before Christmas. We have a suite at a ski resort with all the amenities. We're taking our Christmas presents with us."

"Well, I hope you and Sam have some quiet time for yourselves. I'm sure he'll need to decompress once he gets home."

"I don't think that will be a problem, Sis. You know teenagers today—don't want to be seen with their parents."

As the bus turned off at the Cambridge exit, the tour director briefed everyone on the day's schedule.

"We'll park by the visitor's center," she said. "I suggest you make it your first stop. They'll give you a map with information on all the mannequins, shops, and restaurants in town. Enjoy your afternoon. The courthouse light show starts at 5:00 p.m. It lasts about an hour. Come back to the bus after that; we'll have a hot box lunch catered in by 'Smokin' C's' for the trip home."

As the sisters walked out of the visitor's center with brochures in hand, they were greeted by the sound of horse hooves clip-clopping down the street. Soon a big black steed pulling a sparkling white carriage came into view.

"That's what I want to do first," Sue said. "Remember the buggy rides we took with Grandpa when we visited his farm?"

The trip to Cambridge was just what Sue needed. Walking the streets of the quaint town was good therapy. The stress of raising a family and meeting deadlines all disappeared in the clear, crisp air of southeastern Ohio.

"Well, what do you think, Sue?"

"I'm just amazed by all these mannequins. They are so lifelike. Someone put a lot of work and thought into them."

"Not some*one*, Sue. I read in the brochure that it's all done by a group of volunteers. They work year-round on them. Some of the faces are actual faces of prominent people in the community."

"Amazing," Sue replied. "Simply amazing."

"What was your favorite scene?" Donna asked as they made their way toward the courthouse after the carriage ride.

"I liked the towne crier, Sis. Sam's great-great-grandfather was a towne crier in the old country before he came to the States. Sam has the bell he used to ring."

"How neat! I'd like to see it sometime."

Standing with the merry crowd in front of the courthouse, Sue overheard a conversation between a young couple in front of them.

"Did you see the weather forecast?" the young man asked.

"I did. Hope it's true; we could go skiing next week. The snow machines work okay, but the white fluffy powder's better."

As Sue listened to their conversation, she was leery of asking the couple where they would go skiing around here. Drumming up her courage, she tapped the young lady on the shoulder.

"Excuse me, but I couldn't help overhearing you talk about going skiing. Is there a ski resort in this area? Ah...first let me introduce myself. My name is Sue; this is my sister, Donna. We're visiting from Cleveland. We came to see the Dickens mannequins and the light show."

"Hi! My name is Annie. This is my husband, Ryan. Uh, we don't have a ski resort per se. We ski at Salt Fork Lodge, just east of town. Actually, we ski on the golf course."

"Ski on the golf course?" Sue repeated, puzzled.

"Yeah, the golf course is very hilly. Actually, it's cross country skiing, but it's just the starting point. There are two courses. One starts off "the front nine," as my husband likes to say. It's a 10K course that meanders through the woods and around the lake. Finally, you end up at the lodge. The second one is a 7K course, less demanding but the scenery is spectacular."

"What's this lodge you are talking about?" Sue asked.

"Oh, it's beautiful. It's a large A-frame. It sits on a hill with a spectacular view. *Life Magazine* used it for a cover picture last year. They have a large heated indoor pool, Jacuzzi's in some of the suites, and some of the best dining in the county."

Interesting, Sue thought, *interesting. I wonder why we haven't heard of this place*. The start of the light and music show jarred Sue back to reality.

"What are you thinking, Sue?" Donna interjected. "You have that faraway look in your eyes. I've seen it before—you're up to something."

"I can't believe we haven't heard of this place, Sis. There are buses here from several states. I guess I need to read the vacation flyers in my paper."

All through the light show, Sue couldn't stop thinking about the lodge at the park and the peaceful day she'd just experienced. *Why we are driving hundreds of miles to go skiing when we have all this only two hours away?* she thought.

As the light show ended and the crowd started to disperse, the sisters slowly made their way back to the bus. Passing the visitors center, Sue grabbed Donna's arm.

"Hold the bus." she said. "I want to pick up more brochures."

The bus ride home was quiet and still. Occasionally, the silence was broken by someone coughing or snoring. The sweet smell of barbecued ribs wafted through the cabin.

Sue's mind was racing. *How can I break the news to the family that I would like to go to Cambridge for Christmas instead of the mountains in West Virginia?* Closing her eyes, she leaned her head on Donna's shoulder and was asleep in a minute.

The next few weeks passed quickly. Sue juggled her time between work, planning Christmas vacation, and getting ready for Sam to come home from deployment.

Finally, the day arrived. Sue and the kids rushed to meet Sam as he walked across the tarmac. After a brief ceremony at the local National Guard Armory, they drove home, the first time they had been together as a family for almost a year.

Late that night, Sam told Sue they needed to talk about their future plans. *Oh no!* Sue thought. *Not another deployment.* As the couple sat at the kitchen table with a steaming cup of hot tea spiked with a little brandy, Sam spoke first.

"You know things are winding down in Southwest Asia. The Army is downsizing. They're going to merge our unit with one from Western Pennsylvania."

"What does that mean?" Sue had a worried look on her face.

"It means I'm expendable. They have a full complement of dentists in the unit."

"Expendable?" Sue interjected.

"Yes," Sam said meekly. "It's either relocate, or retire. My new assignment is in my briefcase on the hutch. Would you hand it to me, please?"

As Sue passed the dark leather bag to Sam, her mind raced with the thousands of things relocating meant.

With a serious look, Sam read from the papers in his hand. "Major Sam Patterson, relieved from duty with the 379th Medical Squadron, assigned as chief dental officer to 123 High Street, Evans, Ohio." He laid the papers on the table and looked into

Sue's eyes. "I've decided to retire, Sue. It's time we settled down to be a normal family."

"Oh, Sam," Sue sobbed as tears streamed down her cheeks. "You don't know how I've waited to hear those words. I love it here. I love our house, family, friends. I'm tired of moving."

"Me too, Sue. Me too."

"Well, Major, I have a surprise for you." Sue jumped up to retrieve a stack of papers from her kitchen pantry. "Now, don't get your dander up, hear me out. I cancelled our plans to go skiing in West Virginia and booked a suite at Salt Fork Lodge in Cambridge. You'll love it once you see it, Sam. I hope you're not mad. Guernsey County goes all out for Christmas—train rides, luminaria--you and the kids will love it when you see it."

"I have seen it," Sam said. "I have seen it."

"But…but…how," Sue stuttered. "I just saw it myself."

Sam put his arms around Sue's shoulders and drew her close. "Let me explain. My dental assistant in Afghanistan was from Cambridge. His father is a photographer for the local newspaper, the Jeff something. He sent me pictures and a CD of last year's show. I've been trying to think how to break it to you. I'm tired of traveling. I just want to spend time with you and the kids."

"Oh, that would be wonderful," Sue responded in amazement.

"When two or more agree," Sam uttered softly.

"What's that, Sam?"

"Oh, nothing, just a Bible verse my father used to say. Now, let's go to bed. We can tell the kids in the morning. I think they will like the change once they see the Teen Christmas that's planned for the civic center in town. Now, you know what we haven't done in a long time?"

"No," Sue whispered. "Please tell me."

"Sleep in," Sam whispered in her ear, "Sleep in."

"Well, Major," Sue coquettishly replied, "I think that might be the second thing you get to do that you haven't done for a long time."

The Skaters—1830 London, England, saw the founding of the Skating Club. *Queen Victoria and Prince Albert were fans of ice skating. The sport was very popular with the upper class citizens, who could afford to purchase skates and the latest fashionable attire. This sport grew in popularity and soon became a staple pastime of winter activities among both young and old.*

Back Home for Christmas

HARRIETTE McBRIDE ORR

John Henry stretched as best he could in the crowded plane. It felt so good to be back on terra firma. The trip from Australia had been a long one. Flying into LAX, he had gone through customs. Now arriving in the Columbus airport, John headed straight for the baggage turnstile.

What a striking figure he was—well-tanned from the out-of-doors; his long tall frame comfortably dressed in Levis, custom-tanned boots, and a mouton suede jacket. His wavy white hair was topped off with a fawn-colored beaver Stetson. Drawing stares of admiration, he headed to the Hertz Rent-a-Car counter. After filling out the paperwork, the gal behind the counter produced the keys and escorted him to a pearl white Cadillac Escalade, which his sons had arranged for their dad.

Handling the SUV with ease, he merged onto Interstate 70, heading east to Cambridge. On the ranch, the standard transportation was a four-wheel drive vehicle, an ATV, or a horse. The Browne's could afford whatever they wanted, but never found the need for anything so fancy.

John was beginning to feel the excitement of coming home. He thought back in time to the Cambridge he knew as a kid. Home had been a pleasant place until his mother had passed away when John was a senior in high school. His father had turned into a mean drunk, taking his grieving out on the children. There were episodes of ranting and raving. Sometimes he would strike out at whoever was near.

The drunken rage that caused John to leave Cambridge on the run was a terrible fight with his father. During the week before

Christmas, his dad spent the entire day drinking. He became angry when he couldn't find the Jeffersonian.

"Aaalright," he slurred, "wherrred you put it? You idiots are all the time hiding my things." Picking up a ball bat, he started coming at John and his little sister, Mary. John stepped in front of Mary and yelled, "Stop, Dad! Stop right now!" but his father kept coming. The first thing John knew, he had wrenched the bat from his dad's hands and found himself swinging to fend him off.

One blow struck his father's shoulder, knocking him off balance. He fell forward, striking his head on the corner of the old oak kitchen table. His father just lay there on the kitchen floor with blood gushing from a wound on his head.

Mary screamed, "John, you have killed our father! You've killed our dad!"

Fear gripped John's heart. He shook his father but got no response. "Oh God, what have I done?" Picking up his little sister and grabbing their coats, he ran down the street to Uncle George's house. Frantically, he rang the doorbell. Aunt Margaret opened the door as John shoved Mary inside.

"John, whatever is the matter? Wait!"

"I can't," he shouted as he ran back down the walk. "Call the medics! Dad needs an ambulance! Please take care of Mary."

"John...John," Aunt Margaret pleaded, "please come back."

"I am leaving. I don't have time to explain. Mary will tell you. Call for help!"

Aunt Margaret headed back into the house to the crying Mary.

John managed to make his way to Interstate 70, where he caught a ride with a trucker headed east. He never looked back.

When they reached New York City, the trucker took him right to the docks, where John Henry eventually found a ship headed for Australia that was signing on deckhands.

Working his way across the seas, he laid over in Sidney several times before deciding Australia was where he wanted to stay. John left the ship, hoping to find work. He had been a good deckhand and the captain had written him a letter of recommendation. In Singapore, he had purchased a passport, so he was all set.

Handbills advertising for cowhands on a cattle station near someplace called Waroo were posted all over the docks. He soon found the storefront where they were doing the interviews for the jobs. Giving them his letter of recommendation, he was hired and told to return at 7 a.m. for a ride to the station.

It was late afternoon when they finally pulled in to the gates of the cattle station. From there, it was five miles or more to the house and buildings. John was in awe of everything he heard and saw around him. This was the start of his new life, a life he would grow to love.

He worked hard and soon became a top cowhand. Cambridge was seldom on his mind but he prayed that his sister was doing okay.

The owners of the ranch both took a liking to John and had him spending more and more time at the house for meals. Eventually, he became foreman in charge of the southern herds. Mr. and Mrs. Browne grew to love John and ended up legally adopting him as their son.

He became known throughout Australia as John Henry Browne, one of the wealthiest ranchers in the country. He married Susanna Jackson from the neighboring station and, when both sets of parents passed away, the couple inherited vast acreage and livestock.

They raised four sons, who now ran the stations with their dad. Sue had passed away last year from breast cancer. John Henry had taken her death very hard. They had been married thirty-five years and his love for her was very deep. Now his life was empty without her.

*****

John Henry's cousin, Peter, Uncle George's and Aunt Mary's son, was probate judge of Guernsey County. He had spied John's picture in *USA TODAY*. John was described as a very successful cattle rancher from Australia. The article went on to say how John Henry Browne had become the head of the *Global Organic Animal Foundation for Happy Animals* and was hosting a meeting of this organization at his vast cattle station in Waroo, Australia.

It had been quite a few years since Peter had seen John but he knew from the photo that this was his missing cousin. He looked so much like his father. "What on earth is he doing in Australia?" Peter wondered out loud.

Peter Googled John Henry's name and came up with answers to his query. He immediately sent off a letter to John, telling him how glad he was to find him after all these years. "I am sure this is you; I recognize you from your picture in *USA TODAY*."

When John received the letter, he was a little taken aback when he saw the return address: Guernsey County Probate Court, Cambridge, Ohio. He broke out in a cold sweat. *Are they coming for me after all these years? How on earth did they find me?* With shaking hands, he opened the letter. To his relief, he realized the letter was from his cousin, Peter.

Peter explained that John's father had not been killed, only wounded. He had sobered up and remarried, but only this last year had died of a sudden heart attack. There were no charges pending of any kind.

John's sister, Mary, had married John's best friend, David McBride, and they had three grown children. The letter was full of family news and ended with an invitation for John Henry to come home during the holiday season for a visit.

"Cambridge is decorated like Merry Olde England with Charles Dickens scenes all over town. We are planning a family reunion the weekend of Christmas. Please plan to join us."

John Henry could not believe that, after all these years of hiding, he could now return safely to Ohio. *Oh, how I would love to see Mary and her family.*

Through the years, he had sent money to Mary through untraceable channels. Mary never knew where the money came from but suspected it came from her missing brother.

As his sons gathered for the evening meal, John shared the letter with them and explained why he had left Cambridge. He told them he never dreamed he would be able to return home again.

"Well, Dad," his son, Tom, exclaimed, "there is no reason why you can't do this. We'll get you booked on a plane out of Sydney, and you are out of here. It is winter in Ohio, so you better take some warm clothes. Bud, you get the Cub serviced and we can fly Dad into Sydney."

The boys had made his flight arrangements and contacted Peter.

*****

As John Henry merged off I-70, he headed up Southgate Parkway toward the courthouse. When he got close enough, he could begin to see the light show that happens every night during the Dickens Victorian Village.

As he neared Wheeling Avenue, he sighted the animated skaters on a pond beside Advantage Bank. Across the street were Tiny Tim and Father Christmas mannequins, gracing the courthouse square along with shoppers and real children watching the light show.

Wow! Look at all these people. This is great, he thought.

Cousin Peter had suggested he stay at the Colonel Taylor Inn. At the urging of his sons, he had rented the whole mansion for his stay in Cambridge. With Peter's help, John invited Mary and her family to join him there.

His GPS led him right to the Inn. As he pulled in the driveway blowing his horn, people came running out of the house. He picked Mary out right away. *Oh, she is beautiful and looks so much like Mom.*

Mary ran down the steps, shouting his name. As he stepped out of the car, they hugged and cried for joy at the sight of each other.

"Oh, John, we thought you were dead. I can't believe it is really you. How handsome you are. Just look at you. John, do you remember my David?" As everyone gathered round, Mary introduced her family, and Peter's as well.

"Welcome home, John. We are so glad you are here."

"Thanks to you, Peter, thanks to you."

"Boys, grab his bags and let's go inside," instructed Peter.

The Inn was decorated for Christmas with greenery everywhere. A huge tree ornamented in red and gold graced the entrance hall. Fires were set in the fireplaces in each room, making them a cozy retreat from the December air outside.

The innkeeper, Ms. Carole, had her chef prepare a warm supper for the guests. The table was set with antique flow-blue dishes on a white damask tablecloth. From the sideboard, the chef served a variety of hot soups. Fresh bread and crackers were arrayed on the buffet, with a large selection of warm roast beef and chicken for sandwiches. Dessert was a variety of scrumptious wares from Kennedy's Bakery.

As they were finishing their meal, they heard carolers coming up the walk singing *Joy to the World*. They opened the doors to invite the Victorian-costumed singers inside. Everyone joined in the singing. The carolers' leader, Len Thomas, was invited to play the piano. After a half hour of singing, Len ended the evening with a beautiful rendition of *O Holy Night*. Some of the children had fallen asleep, so everyone decided it was bedtime.

As the families drifted up to bed, John and Mary settled in the parlor, where they talked until the wee hours of the morning. John Henry checked his e-mail before he turned in. There were notes from the boys. They had made sure that the Inn had wi-fi and Cousin Peter had set up Skype so the families could see each other.

The next morning when John Henry came downstairs there was a scrumptious English breakfast buffet set up in the large dining room. He spent time getting reacquainted with Mary's husband and their boys.

As they finished their breakfast they decided it would be nice to tour downtown Cambridge. Ms. Carole arranged for horse-drawn carriages to be at their disposal all day.

By the time they got everyone loaded up, a light snow had begun to fall and they broke into *Jingle Bells*. People could hear them coming and stopped to watch as the carriages rushed by. At the top of Main Street, they left the carriages and did a walking tour, stopping at each Dickens scene, reading the plaques and taking pictures. When they came to the Olde Curiosity Shoppe, they all dressed in Victorian garb at the Imagination Station and took more pictures, with Charles Dickens and the Duke and Duchess of Cambridge.

John had not experienced such a good time since his Susanna had passed away. He looked around at everyone talking and laughing and took a moment to thank the Lord above for bringing him home.

He sent a media text to the boys, showing them all of the happenings on the courthouse square. John Henry and Mary posed with Tiny Tim as Peter took videos.

Buying hot chocolate from the street vendors for everyone, John Henry offered a toast: "To family. To home. God bless us, every one!"

John Henry texted his sons: *Ths is 1 dickens of a Christmas. Mry Christmas. Mry Christmas to all. C u soon. Lv, ur dad.*

Out on the Town—*Dickens became engaged to Catherine Hogarth in 1835. The couple married on 2 April 1836 and established their home in London.*

THE GREAT CANDY WRAPPER CAPER

JOY L. WILBERT ERSKINE

Joey Newell tiptoed past his parents' bedroom in stocking feet, holding his breath. Muffled snoring attested to his father's drift into dreamland, his head tucked under the covers. Listening closely, Joey perceived with relief the gentle sigh of his mother's breathing and, reassured, drew a slow breath himself. It was two o'clock on Christmas morning and he'd been waiting patiently for everyone to fall asleep. Even as excited as he was, it'd been pretty tough for the seven-year-old to stay awake so long.

The bathroom nightlight emitted sufficient illumination to see him past the room his two sisters, Annie and Julie, shared. Once on the staircase, though, he almost tripped over Barker, the little Yorkshire terrier Dad always referred to as "the dust mop that wanted to be a dog."

"Darn it, Barker," he whispered. "That's about the dumbest place you could pick to lay down." The dog humphed and yawned, then followed sleepily behind Joey, hopping from tread to tread two paws at a time.

Juggling four gaily-wrapped packages, Joey led the way into the living room. The space was illuminated mostly by a big bay window overlooking a prime view of Cambridge's main thoroughfare. Wheeling Avenue, outlined with lantern lights like a reindeer runway, was decorated for the holiday season with festive wreaths and colorful banners. Christmas scenes straight out of a Dickens novel populated the sidewalks, making the street seem crowded with people even at this late hour. Joey paused to peek out at the scenes on the street, letting his imagination take flight.

"You can almost hear them talking to each other, Barker," he whispered, his voice filled with all the awe of a child on Christmas Eve. "Look at that man, carrying packages, just like me! I bet they have wonderful stories to tell, if we could only listen close enough."

Freshly fallen snow and the resultant hush made it seem possible to do just that. A movement caught Joey's eye. *Did that one just wave at me?* Not quite believing, Joey watched intently, waiting for further signs of life. All was still. Slowly, his attention turned to the twinkling lights of the Christmas tree, glittering like stardust.

A majestic ten-foot presence, the tree filled the corner of the room, its dancing lights piercing the darkness with magical bits of vibrant color. Underneath were nestled what seemed to Joey like a million packages wrapped in bright Christmas colors.

"Gosh, Barker! Look at all the packages! Santa's already been here," Joey squealed. He slapped his hand over his mouth, his eyes big as moon pies, remembering his slumbering family upstairs. He stood motionless, his ears straining for the sounds of awakening...but all remained quiet.

Chattering softly, he carefully added his gifts to the piles of presents Santa had delivered. "I can't wait to see their faces in the morning," he whispered excitedly to Barker. "I saved my allowance for six months. This'll be the best Christmas ever."

Joey let his eyes wander around the room, taking everything in. Christmas gave a magical glow to the moonlit scene, catching him in its spell. Sleepily, he snuggled into the overstuffed chair by the fireplace. Tiny colored lights flashed rhythmically along the decorative fir and pinecone roping draped on the massive stone mantle. Candy canes, bonbons, and small teddy bears peeked over the tops of five red Christmas stockings, hanging as heavy as Joey's red-rimmed eyes. The evening fire was cold in the hearth, but the warm chair worked its own brand of enchantment on one very tired little boy.

Before the sun cleared the horizon, Annie and Julie flew into Joey's room chattering like the two calling birds in *The Twelve Days of Christmas.*

"Wake up, Joey! It's Christmas!" Quickly realizing her brother wasn't in his bed, Annie declared to her younger sister, "I bet he crawled in with Mom and Dad. Let's go wake them up!" Running down the hall and through their parents' bedroom door, they flung themselves on the bed, bouncing and giggling. "Merry Christmas, wake up everyone!" Mom and Dad groaned simultaneously. Dad added, "Girls, go back to bed. It's too early."

Little Julie was the first to notice. "Where's Joey?" she asked. "Mamma, Joey's not in his room, and he's not here either." Startled instantly awake, Mom and Dad both leaped in terror from their bed. Grabbing robes, they raced in tandem to Joey's bedroom, the girls close behind.

Dad threw back the bedcovers, but the bed was empty. Dropping to her knees, Mom fumbled around on the floor beneath the bed. A lone Power Ranger fell into her grasp, but no Joey. Tears began welling up in her eyes.

"Downstairs! He must be downstairs," reasoned Dad. Rushing to the landing, he took the steps two at a time. As he turned the corner into the living room, he skidded to a stop and whispered back up to his wife, "Here he is, Honey. Fast asleep in the chair by the fireplace."

Eyes still moist, she descended the stairs to look for herself, hugging her daughters close to her side. It was a tender picture…a wee little boy and his dog curled up together, basking in the twinkling lights, waiting for Christmas morning, and…what was that white stuff all over the floor? The girls tiptoed closer to see. Annie bravely reached out to touch. "It's paper, Mamma," she reported in a whisper. "Candy wrappers! Joey's been eating the candy Santa brought!"

"Alright, sleepyhead," she suddenly crowed. "Wake up!" She and Julie jumped onto the chair, bringing a yelp from Barker and a sigh of protest from their brother. Joey, rubbing his knuckles into his eyes, tried to wake up with little success. His sisters pulled at his pajamas until he was on his feet. "You started Christmas without us," protested Julie. "Why didn't you wait for us?"

"Yes, young man," intoned Dad in his best unhappy father voice. "Why didn't you wait?"

"I did wait, Dad. I fell asleep watching the lights," Joey said. His eyes fell on the candy wrappers. And then on Barker.

"Barker! Did you eat the Christmas candy?" he questioned sternly. Barker grinned a doggy grin, the long hair on his stubby tail mopping the chair cushion in happiness.

"Looks like Barker's the culprit all right," agreed Mom. "But how? The stockings are all still hanging on the mantle." Inspecting closer, she added, "The candy's missing only from the tops of the stockings. How is that possible?"

"Let's see if he'll demonstrate for us," proposed Dad. He fished some candy out of one stocking to refill another to the top to tempt the dog to repeat the infraction. "This ought to be good," he chuckled. "Where's the video recorder? Let's sit quietly for a few minutes and see what happens."

It didn't take long. Barker watched the proceedings with interest and then unselfconsciously performed a routine he'd obviously perfected during the night by the light of the Christmas tree. Jumping atop the back of the chair, he stood up on his hindquarters and sniffed. The distance from the chair to the mantle was a little chancy for such a tiny dog, but the family watched as Barker expertly assessed the risk. Before their very eyes, he leaped like a little lion across the chasm, trotted daintily along the mantle to the full stocking, dropped his nose intrepidly over the edge, and carefully nipped the tail of a candy wrapper with his teeth.

Planting a paw on the opposite end of the wrapper, he gave it a gentle tug, releasing the soft confection onto the mantle. Then he let the wrapper drop to the floor. Barker nudged the sweet to a safe place, repeating the performance several more times. The family laughed uproariously at the little critter's ingenuity. When he'd gathered all he could reach, Barker transferred the booty to the chair, jumping to and from the mantle with practiced ease. Satisfied, he settled in comfort and safety to wolf down his treats.

"Barker! Bad boy!" Joey unconvincingly scolded in his best unhappy master voice. "Now you're gonna be sick, you dumb dog."

"Actually, he's a pretty darn smart dog, Joey, but you're right, you'd better put him out now," Dad wisely advised.

A few months later, the Newell family all agreed that it *had* been the best Christmas ever. Barker, fully recovered from a bad bellyache, accompanied his people to a taping of "America's Funniest Home Videos" and won the grand prize—but he never again burgled the bonbons.

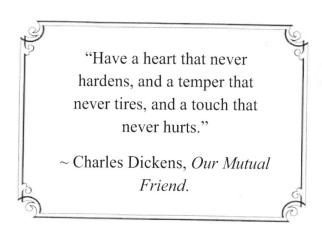

"Have a heart that never hardens, and a temper that never tires, and a touch that never hurts."

~ Charles Dickens, *Our Mutual Friend.*

School Time—*Victorians were determined to provide the best possible schooling for their children. There were many fine British grammar and private boarding schools. However, the poor classes were not afforded the same privileges. As a result, by 1860, one third of all British men and women lacked the ability to read and write. Local educator Anne Stillion was the model for the face of the teacher in this scene.*

JINGLE BELL BUS

BEVERLY WENCEK KERR

"Oh, what fun it is to ride in a bus with jingle bells," sang Harold and his wife, Lucille, as he placed his favorite string of jingle bells over the mirror of his bus...school bus, that is. In the forty years that Harold had driven school bus, he always decorated it for the Christmas season.

The jingle bells he hung over the mirror had been passed down in his family from his grandmother. Their jingle meant more to him than any other Christmas decoration. It also brought back memories of those times spent at the farm long ago when he helped his sister build the perfect snowman, complete with eyes of coal, a carrot nose, and a black top hat on his head. Completing the day were exhilarating sled rides down the back pasture over the crisp snow.

Tomorrow Harold would drive the first grade from Liberty School to Dickens Victorian Village, so he wanted his Christmas decorations on a little earlier than usual this year. Lucille helped him decorate the side windows of the bus with snow scenes. Snow along the window bottoms made a perfect setting for several snowmen to be placed along the windows. When the children looked out, it would always appear to be a winter wonderland. On the front of the bus, Harold secured a three-foot wreath with a shiny red bow and blinking lights. Ready to roll!

Sounds of excited children greeted him as the Jingle Bell Bus pulled up at Liberty School in the morning. There were twenty-five six- and seven-year-olds, eager to visit the streets of Cambridge. Once they all hopped aboard with their teacher, Mrs. Bell, Harold shouted, "Merry Christmas! Let's all sing *Jingle Bells*." Down the road they bounced along on the Jingle Bell Bus while singing a merry tune.

Jingle Bells, Jingle Bells
Jingle all the way.

The song spilled from the big yellow bus, which carried many students—some who had never been to downtown Cambridge at this time of year. Mary, a favorite of all the students, had never seen the mannequins before, or knew the stories behind these characters on Wheeling Avenue. Since she had never been on a field trip, the excited Mary and her blond curls bounced along with the bus. Even though she felt a little sick this morning, she didn't tell her mother or her teacher. She would pretend she was okay in order to see the Dickens mannequins.

As the bus started down Wheeling Avenue, children would call out anytime they spotted another mannequin scene along the street.

"There's a lady mailing something at the post office."

"Look at that woman begging for food."

"That looks like people singing."

"There's Santa Claus in a green coat!"

"Mrs. Bell, I see a man in chains right in front of the restaurant."

Peering from the school bus at the characters along the street,

Tommy pressed his nose against the window. No one wanted to share a seat with Tommy, who wore ragged clothes and sometimes smelled like a wet puppy dog—or worse. This poor child wanted to be friends, but the other children just wrinkled up their noses when Tommy approached. *Maybe for Christmas this year a friend will appear*, hoped Tommy.

When they arrived at the Dickens Welcome Center, two ladies dressed in long skirts, warm capes, and beautiful hats met the students. They planned to take the students for a walk down Wheeling Avenue past the mannequins and explain some of the stories about them.

Twenty-five bouncing first graders were dressed in warm coats and toboggans. Most even had gloves because it was a cold day with a little snow on the ground—just perfect for a walk down Wheeling Avenue! As they walked up the street, the Victorian lady explained that the man in the green coat was actually called Father Christmas in the time of Charles Dickens. Father Christmas was very similar to Santa Claus of present time.

Mary lagged at the end of the group now, back where Tommy usually stayed to avoid the rest of the class. The walk down the street tired out this sick little girl. But she still trudged on.

The beggar lady scene showed a poor lady who held a basket for food or money for her children. Often the beggar lady made up stories in hopes that people might give her something. She touched their cloaks as she told them, "My husband fell off the roof and broke his leg so he can't work," or "My little girl has a high fever and needs some medicine." Hopefully, someone would help her family.

The children enjoyed the stories as they went down the street. One scene which really grasped their interest was "Naughty and Nice." Here a naughty little boy tried to pull the pigtail of a nice little girl. They understood the teasing that children have always enjoyed. Their laughter rang down the street as the guide told the story.

"School Time" was another scene, depicting a teacher with the typical bell on her desk but also a lantern to light the room on gloomy days. The children in that scene were dressed in warm plaid coats, caps, and warm scarves. These were definitely the rich children of that time. Poorer children during the time of Charles Dickens had no coats and often didn't even have shoes to wear in the wintertime. Sometimes they tied rags around their feet for a little warmth.

Finally, the walk down the street was finished. The children were eager to move inside where it was warmer. As they entered the Cambridge Visitors Bureau, they were greeted by more Victorian ladies who told them about the life of children during the time of Charles Dickens and about today's Dickens Victorian Village. As they settled into comfortable chairs, they were first shown how the heads were made for the mannequins. Since children enjoy working with papier-mâché, this piqued their curiosity.

While the children learned about the games played during the time of Charles Dickens, Mrs. Bell was busy counting heads to make certain all of the children were present. She smiled to herself, noticing how clever it was for the Dickens Victorian Village to have surprised them with three authentic-looking children dressed in Victorian clothes. They wore plaid coats and scarves that were not like the warm winter garb of the children in her class at all. They sat with her class and enjoyed the stories that were told.

As she continued counting her twenty-five students, twice she came up with the figure of twenty-seven, which included the three Victorian additions. A student was missing! Her eyes scanned the class list rapidly as panic set in.

Mary, where is Mary? Where could she be? The anxious teacher jumped from her seat. Her voice quivered when she spoke. "Excuse me, but I must interrupt. Is Mary here?" No hands were raised and the children started talking among themselves. "Does anyone remember seeing Mary on our walk down the street?"

Shy little Tommy raised his hand and quietly offered, "Last I saw her, she was standing by the apple cart out on the sidewalk. She didn't look like she was feeling good, but she told me to go on. She'd catch up. Think she was wanting to get an apple for you, Mrs. Bell."

Reaching out to grasp Tommy's hand, Mrs. Bell requested in a voice filled with panic, "Come with me, Tommy." Out the door they flew. Up the street ran Tommy, with Mrs. Bell close behind, to the scene where Tommy had last seen his missing classmate. There they found Mary curled up under the apple cart fast asleep. With the apple cart over her, Mary was barely noticeable since she was so small.

"Mary, Mary," coaxed the perplexed Mrs. Bell, gently touching the child's shoulder. "Can you get up? What's the matter?"

"I'll be fine, Mrs. Bell," answered the groggy little girl. "Please don't make me go home. I want to stay on this field trip. Please!"

By this time, a kind gentleman from Dickens Victorian Village had arrived at the scene to drive Mary, Tommy, and their teacher back to the Center. Tommy was a hero for having remembered where Mary stopped. Both Mary and Tommy received a round of applause from their classmates.

Before they left the Center that morning, the guides gave each student a red ribbon with a jingle bell to hang around their neck while they all sang *Jingle Bells*. Now *that* would be a nice surprise for Harold when they climbed back on his bus.

Out front, the Jingle Bell Bus was waiting for Mrs. Bell's class. Harold's cheeks were rosy with laughter as he watched the children boarding. How he enjoyed seeing the jingle bells hanging around their necks. This was going to be a fun ride home with everyone singing *Jingle Bells* again...this time with accompaniment.

Tommy, true to form, stayed at the end of the line. When he got on the bus, several voices called out to him now, "Tommy, sit with me. I've got room here." But Tommy just shook his head and said with a sparkle in his eyes, "Not this time. Mary asked me to sit with her." And that's just what he did. Tommy had found a new friend, the best Christmas present ever.

* * * * *

The following weekend, Mary convinced her parents to go downtown so she could again see the Dickens mannequins, now that she was feeling better. Before leaving home, Mary placed the red ribbon with jingle bell around her neck. Jingling all the way, she skipped down the street from one Dickens scene to the next. When she came to the scene, "School Time," she suddenly stopped and carefully looked at the figures.

"Mom, Dad, these kids look like the ones that sat with us when our class was in town. They even have on clothes like them, but their faces looked happier that day."

Then she noticed it. "Look, they each one have a jingle bell ribbon like mine. Maybe they really are the same kids."

Mom and Dad exchanged a wink and a smile. Mary reached up and shook the girl's jingle bell along with her own and bounced while she sang *Jingle Bells.*

Were they really the same children that were on the field trip? You never know what the magic of Christmas can create at Dickens Victorian Village!

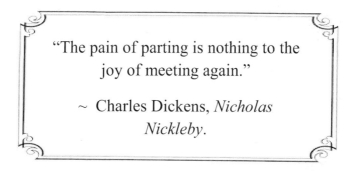

"The pain of parting is nothing to the joy of meeting again."

~ Charles Dickens, *Nicholas Nickleby.*

RDW at Dickens Universal

RDW at Dickens Universal

THE
RAINY DAY
WRITERS'
BIOGRAPHIES

JAMES ASP, a single parent, considers himself a Quaker City native. Though born in a suburb of Cleveland during the Nixon administration, he moved to Guernsey County as a very young boy. A 1988 graduate of Buckeye Trail, he immediately enlisted in the U.S. Navy, where he was permanently stationed aboard a fast frigate in Pearl Harbor, Hawaii. After honorable discharge, James moved to Cambridge and became actively involved in many community organizations including parental groups and the Guernsey County Veteran's Council, where he regularly performs military funerals. James loves to write and to touch the lives of others through humor and kindness.

Retirement for **SAMUEL D. BESKET** brought opportunities for exploring new interests and doing things he didn't have time for when he was working. Currently, he writes a column for The Daily Jeffersonian, drives part-time for the Disabled American Veterans, and is a member of Rainy Day Writers. He is an avid reader and is a student of American History. He lists *The Longest Raid of the Civil War* by Lester Horwitz as his favorite book and *The Godfather* as his favorite movie.

RICK BOOTH wrote computer code for two decades before finally taking a college instructor's advice to try his hand at English. His first book on high-performance computing, 1997's *Inner Loops*, was well received for its mix of solid code and readable prose. Intel subsequently recruited his talents for another technical tome in 2001. Returning from the East Coast to Cambridge, his hometown, in 2007, Rick now enjoys writing *entirely* in English in a variety of genres, including fiction and humor. He currently authors a monthly history column for Now & Then magazine, yet still yearns to write Android apps.

JOY L. WILBERT ERSKINE is a California transplant to Cambridge, but has lived here now for over 20 years. A former university medical school administrative assistant, she is also mother of two and grandmother of six. She has since her youth had a serious writing bent, but life had other ideas. At last retired, Joy is now able to indulge in her passion for writing. She coordinates the efforts of the Rainy Day Writers, writes columns for The Daily Jeffersonian and short stories for the Rainy Day Writers, and has aspirations of publishing her own work in the next few years.

From childhood, **MARTHA F. JAMAIL** has been an avid lover of art and writing. After a 32-year teaching career, she now devotes more time to art and writing projects. For the past eight years, Martha has volunteered with Dickens Victorian Village. As an artist she helped create unique character heads for the life-size scenes on display during the Christmas season. Now a one-year member of the Rainy Day Writers, Martha was excited about the selection of Dickens Victorian Village as the topic for their new book. She chose two of her favorite characters to bring to life in her stories.

BEVERLY J. JUSTICE, a Cambridge, Ohio, native, graduated from Kent State University with a B.A. in English. She also attended the former Muskingum Area Technical College, now known as Zane State. Her poetry and short stories have been published in *The Daily Jeffersonian* and national publications, including *Cat Fancy* magazine. Her favorite contemporary authors are Dean Koontz, Stephen King, and Mitch Albom. She cites Henry David Thoreau as one of the greatest influences in her life. Her interests include the American Civil War, animal welfare, and physical fitness.

BEVERLY WENCEK KERR finds pleasure in assisting at Dickens Victorian Village. Through her involvement with a group of retired teachers, *The Educational Side of Dickens* has reached hundreds of local students. Her play, *A Magical World of Dickens*, gave new life to the Dickens' mannequins. Being a step-on tour guide allows her to share stories of Dickens and Guernsey County with many visitors. Beverly also finds great pleasure in exploring wherever she happens to go, and shares her adventures at *www.gypsyroadtrip.com*. Above all, family and friends are the most important part of her life.

DICK METHENEY is a retired steel mill worker turned full-time farmer. He is an avid reader and book collector, and has been a factory worker, apprentice precision grinder, landscaper, horse trainer, cattle rancher, school bus driver, and income tax preparer. He and his wife, Alice, live on a farm near Quaker City, Ohio, where Dick carves out time each day to devote to writing. He is the author of four books: *If It Is God's Will*, *Santana's Revenge*, *Carter's Revenge*, and *Escaping Strange Creek*. In his spare time, he enjoys the occasional hunting trip in Montana.

HARRIETTE MCBRIDE ORR is a native of Guernsey County. She attended Cambridge schools and is retired from Champion Spark Plug. Christmas has always been a favorite time of the year for Harriette. She loves volunteering for the Dickens Victorian Village in downtown Cambridge and organizing the Cambridge Main Street Christmas Steeple Walk. Writing short stories has become a favorite pastime. Her stories are drawn on life experiences with a little imagination and humor thrown in. She hopes you enjoy this latest presentation by the Rainy Day Writers and, to everyone, may you have a "Dickens of a Christmas."

DONNA J. LAKE SHAFER has always enjoyed "people watching" and sometimes mentally invents little fictional histories about them for her own amusement. But putting thoughts and feelings into mannequins to bring them to life for this book was a daunting prospect. Inspired by a delightful visit to Dickens Universal and the creativity of so many dedicated and talented volunteers, she roused her Christmas Spirit, put pen to paper, and went to work on her stories for *A Dickens of a Christmas*. She hopes readers enjoy the results.

DWAIN WILLIAMS enjoys writing from a perspective found deep in the heart of Appalachia—down home, folksy, plain and truthful, at times touching on the historical—that's his approach to storytelling and to life. A self-employed carpenter and wood craftsman, he makes his home in a quiet country setting south of Quaker City, Ohio, a perfect spot for receiving inspiration for his writing. *A Dickens of a Christmas* was a bit of a stretch for Dwain, but he hopes his story will draw his readers deeper into the true meaning and spirit of Christmas.

JERRY WOLFROM is now in his 55th year as a reporter, editor, publisher, and freelance writer. While at Bowling Green State University, he was voted Top College Columnist in Ohio. Later he received the Golden Scissors Award for outstanding journalism. In 1988, BGSU inducted Jerry into the Journalism Hall of Fame there. He prefers humor and outdoor writing. His freelance work has taken him to eight different countries.

The Rainy Day Writers: A Dickens of a Writing Group: Standing L to R: Martha F. Jamail, James Asp, Donna J. Lake Shafer, Dick Metheney, Samuel D. Besket, Harriette McBride Orr, Rick Booth, Beverly Wencek Kerr, Beverly J. Justice, Dwain Williams; Seated: Joy L. Wilbert Erskine. Not pictured: Jerry Wolfrom.

A GREAT BIG RAINY DAY THANKS
to loyal and supportive friend,
Michael Neilson.

Made in the USA
Charleston, SC
17 November 2013